# AGAINST THE ROPES

## A FIGHTER ROMANCE

SKARA GRAY

## EXPLICIT CONTENT FOR 18+

I mark this original piece of work as mature and appropriate for audiences 18+ due to sexual scenes, cursing, and limited violence. I am always open to feedback about all aspects of my work but please keep this in mind.

## GET A FREE BOOK!

Join Skara Gray's Mailing List to get a FREE book as well as news on upcoming releases and exclusive bonus chapters!

## OTHER BOOKS BY SKARA GRAY

*Fighter Series*

In His Corner: A fighter romance

Below The Belt: A fighter romance

*Standalone*

Seeing Red: A billionaire romance

## AGAINST THE ROPES

Nico Chavez doesn't get lucky breaks. He's from the roughest part of Boston and has been dealt a shitty hand. With two younger sisters to care for and no one to help him, he turns to underground fighting to make ends meet. When a match lands him up against the area's top fighter, Rhett Jaggar, he knows he's got a shot at fighting for real.

When Rhett retires from the ring, he takes on Nico as his protégé, the opportunity of a lifetime. After a year of training under the watchful eye of Rhett and the legendary Coach Barry, Nico is ready to enter his biggest fighting circuit yet. He's determined to make a name for himself and his sisters.

Meredith Barry has been acting out. From drugs to bad boys to skipping class, she's hellbent on making all the wrong choices. When she gets suspended from college for the semester, her mother sends her to live with her estranged father, a veteran boxing coach in Boston. Meredith is already angry at the world, but the thought of leaving sunny California to go live with a dad she barely knows has her blood boiling.

When the beautiful but icy redhead sets foot in her dad's boxing gym, no one can believe that she's Coach Barry's daughter. Meredith has no idea what to expect from this fighting world, but when her dad gives her the opportunity to be Nico's temporary tour manager and travel for the next few months, all Meredith sees is a way to run from her past.

Nico doesn't want to be that guy who goes after the coach's irresistible daughter. He's trained too hard and has too much at stake for reckless distractions. But when someone from Meredith's past comes back to haunt her, Nico may find that this is one fight he can't ignore.

Can be read as a standalone fighter romance, or as a follow-on story to *In His Corner*. [50,000 to 70,000 words]

## COVER ART

Cover image is professionally created with proper image licensing.

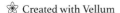 Created with Vellum

# 1

## MEREDITH

"You know, Meredith, if this was your first and only offense, we may be able to agree to a month-long suspension. But you've been in my office nearly once a week this entire semester. I can't give you any more chances." The University Chancellor steepled her fingers on the surface of her desk, a concerned and disappointed look on her softly wrinkled face. "I don't know what's changed for you, Meredith. Your test scores last year were among the top 12.5% of our freshman student body. Your entry exam was a standout. I suggest you do a little self-reflection over the next four months."

My head whipped up from staring at her hands on the desk to face the Chancellor directly. "Over the next four months?"

"You're suspended, Meredith. You can come back in the fall. Pending a re-evaluation and absolutely no trouble with the law. Not even a jaywalking ticket."

"But...you can't! I mean, I pay to be here!" I placed my palms on the desk, trying to steady myself.

"I'm afraid, Miss Barry, that I can. And to be more accurate, your parents pay for you to be here based on your most recent tuition invoice. Your current credits will remain on file and if you still want to graduate in four years, you'll have the option of taking summer and online classes." The Chancellor leaned back in her traditional, stuffy leather chair, watching me closely. "I suggest you focus more on your inner self. Perhaps some therapy sessions would be good."

"Yeah, easy for you to say." I stood up from my seat, throwing my long, dark red hair behind my shoulders as I sashayed angrily toward the office door.

"I wish you the best, Meredith, I truly do." I didn't respond. I needed to get the hell out of here, and fast. I wasn't about to let some old, ivory-tower Chancellor see any hot tears stream down my face. I wasn't sad, I was frustrated. I was pissed. At least, that was my internal dialogue and I was sticking to it. My mom was going to freaking murder me.

"Woah, Meredith, wait up!" I heard a familiar voice behind me on the university lawn but I kept walking. I needed to be alone. Preferably under my sheets in my dorm room where it was dark and quiet and I could be left to think about what the fuck I was going to do for the next four months in peace. *Four freaking months!*

"Hey," my friend Toni reached my shoulder and was out of breath. I didn't relent in my pace. "What is up with you, Red?"

"Don't call me that." I hated that nickname. I'd told Toni a million times that I wanted it to die in high school where it started. Toni and I grew up together, one of the pros and cons of going to a state school in the same place where you grew up. California colleges plus amazing year-round weather made it too hard to leave my childhood state. Even if it meant I couldn't fully recreate my image like I'd wanted to. I had been a little bit of a nerd in high school. Quiet, focused on my grades, shy around boys. I hadn't been some loner in the lunchroom or anything, but I definitely wasn't keen on getting attention. The summer before college I made a pact with myself to change that. I didn't want to go into my young adult life as the wallflower or the observer. I'd followed through on my commitment all of freshman year. I joined a sorority, was involved in academic clubs, went to parties and made more fair-weather friends than I could remember. Too bad sophomore year wasn't going nearly as well. In fact, it was a dumpster fire. But Toni didn't need to know that.

"Look, I just...I think I failed a test and I need some space. Sorry." I kept walking toward my dorm, hoping the lame excuse would get her off my back.

"You? Failing a test? Shit, that is bad." Toni sighed and touched my shoulder. "Text me if you need anything. I'll see ya around."

I looked down in response to a ping on my phone. Official emails from the University Chancellor's office. Geez, they wasted no time. I opened the attachment and it outlined the terms of my suspension, written out in perfectly formal and cordial language that was really just masking a big, giant, *"fuck you, failure"*, which honestly would have been easier to swallow.

The Chancellor's words bounced painfully back and forth in mind: *I suggest you focus more on your inner self. Perhaps some therapy sessions would be good.* If only she freaking knew. My inner self was gone. Broken. Leaving me alone with my own thoughts for four months was probably the most dangerous sentence she could grant me. But she didn't know that. No one did. And no one was going to find out.

I glanced back at the email, the words blurring and magnifying through my restrained tears. I got to the steps of my dorm building when I noticed I wasn't the only recipient of the email.

*Shit, they sent it to my mother too!*

As if on cue, my phone started to buzz and I outwardly groaned in frustration. I couldn't even have five freaking minutes alone with the news that my life was over before my mother was already calling to chastise me even more. If I ignored her call, I would just be delaying the inevitable and the painful. I took a deep breath and hit 'accept.'

"Hi, mom…"

"Meredith Elizabeth Barry! I am getting in my car right now and driving to campus to pick you up. You had better have an explanation for this because I am absolutely livid right now! What am I going to tell your stepfather?" I heard the ding of her Mercedes as she climbed into the driver's seat, already huffing out in exasperation. Of course her first thought was about my stepfather. It was like my mother was embarrassed of me whenever I was less than perfect. And well, this was like one hundred million miles from perfect.

"I don't know, Mom, tell him that I'm a fuck up."

"Meredith! Language! I raised a young lady. What on Earth has gotten into you?"

Part of me wanted to tell her. Just say it in plain language, out in the open. But she wouldn't believe me. No one would. She already saw me as a failure, did I really want to risk her branding me as a liar too?

"I'll go pack my things." I hung up the phone and angrily wiped the tears from my eyes.

## 2

---

## NICO

"Hey, Nico!" I heard Rhett's voice call out behind me. The sweat dripped into my eyes as I slammed my fists into the cracked leather punching bag, one thud after another.

"Yeah, Coach?" My throat was hoarse. I didn't even know how long I'd been at this today. Maybe five hours deep already? Time warped when I stepped into this gym.

"Hey, I'm still the 'Coach' around here." Coach Barry came over to stand beside Rhett, his bald head gleaming under the gym's spotlights. Coach Barry had been Rhett's coach before Rhett retired from the ring. Rhett had been the best of the best. The king of the underground. I was gunning for his throne. But I was still a long way from it.

"Why don't you take a rest from the bag and come up into my office to sign some paperwork?" Coach Barry addressed me before he turned to head toward his office. Rhett nodded quickly, telling me without words to hurry my ass up. My chest was still heaving slightly from exertion, and every inch of my olive tan skin was slick with sweat.

"Take a seat, Nico." Coach was behind his desk, his

glasses perched on his nose. I didn't move when I saw Ava standing behind him. She was all caramel brown hair and feminine curves. She looked like one of those girls from a TV commercial.

"Hey." Rhett came into the office behind me, slapping his hand hard against the back of my head.

"What? I didn't even say anything!" I threw up my hands in my defense, looking at Rhett.

"Yeah, but you were thinking it." Rhett stalked over to Ava and kissed her possessively. There wasn't anyone within miles of this gym who didn't know that Ava was Rhett's girl. He made that shit *known*. I'd never go for a girl like that anyway. Girls that pretty make me nervous as hell. She wasn't simply hot or sexy. She was gorgeous, like something porcelain or whatever. That and me just didn't mix. Never had. Not sure how Rhett managed to get his way with her but that woman loved him to death. I fidgeted on my feet, slightly uncomfortable at their display of affection.

"Sorry, Nico." Ava gave me a soft smile and pushed Rhett back gently. "I'll leave you all to the contracts. Let me know when we need to start planning travel and staffing details." She flashed me another feminine smile and I nodded awkwardly in response.

"Are you going to sit or just keep standing there like a statue?" Coach Barry threw his glasses down on the table and I moved in quickly toward him, taking a seat across the desk. "This is a big contract. We're talking a full-on, legit sponsored, no underground tournament. Even the legendary Rhett over here," Coach Barry jerked his thumb at Rhett who was leaning cockily against the wall, "couldn't manage to keep his nose clean enough to fight in these types of events. There's no drugs, no booze, no prostitutes. And by 'no' I mean the tour will be crawling with that shit but you can't even so much as think about touching it. Do you understand what I'm telling you?"

I looked between Coach and Rhett, nodding fervently. To be honest, I wasn't fucking sure. I'd never left Boston. I'd barely left my neighborhood in my twenty-four years of life, except to come to this gym to train. And all that wasn't to say I had been sheltered. Far from it. My younger sisters and I grew up in foster care, bouncing between displaced family members and temporary homes. I started fighting because there was a wild energy inside of me. And I kept fighting because I was good at it. And being good at something meant you could get paid for it. So, no, I didn't know what traveling the country would be like or how many drugs would really cross my path. But I was desperate, hungry. Coach Barry could've told me there'd be fucking dragons on the boxing tour and I'd still have gone. But that wasn't the kind of shit I needed to be admitting out loud.

"Rhett and I will alternate flying in for major fights. We will get you a full-time tour manager who will oversee your day-to-day. We'd come along for the whole tour, but Rhett has Ava who'll be holding down the gym on her own and I have..." Coach sighed and removed his glasses, setting them on the desk with a thud, "I might have my kid staying with me on and off for a few months so we will just have to be flexible." I nodded quickly, the details blurring as I stared at my name, Nico Chavez, signed in apprehensive cursive next to a six figure contract that could change my life and my sisters'.

"First fight is in six weeks. You've been training for over a year and it's paid off. You're ready for this from a technical fighting perspective." Rhett moved closer to the desk, choosing his words carefully. "But you're still young. Not too young to not be strong enough but not old enough to know the culture, the mental game. If I could teach it to you I would. But it's just one of those things you'll have to figure out on your own. And it's broken great fighters before. Remember that." Rhett's face was serious. He wasn't trying to scare or threaten me. He had shown me over the last year that his intentions with my success were genuine. He saw an electricity in me that he wanted to cultivate and I couldn't be a more eager student. But, I still had the sense that while we'd both been through shit in our lives, his was more of the seedier variety while mine was just plain ol' bad luck. Going on this tour and really living the life of a traveling fighter would probably help me better understand Rhett and his past temptations.

"I'm ready." I stood up from my seat, having signed all the necessary paperwork. My hands were itching to get back to the bag. Coach Barry smiled at me but his expression was tired.

"Yeah, son, that's what they all say. The real test will be in a few months once you're in the thick of it. But we believe in you."

## 3

## MEREDITH

I felt my phone ring in my hand but there was no point in answering it. I knew my mom and her Mercedes were parked outside of my dorm. I allowed myself one more outward groan before I grabbed my bags and fixed a look of stone-cold apathy on my face. Tears wouldn't get me anywhere at this point. I was way too screwed.

"Meredith! My god, I almost crashed driving here I'm so angry with you. I just got off the phone with the Chancellor who detailed for me that you had drugs, DRUGS, on campus! And that they are nearly confident you were selling them! Why on god's green earth would a perfectly spoiled and well-cared for young lady like yourself be selling drugs?" My mom's pale blue irises were nearly leaping out of her face, the fine lines around her eyes deepening with emotion. *Was all she ever thought about reputation and money?*

"I'm sorry, Mom." I moved past her and threw my bags into the trunk before sliding into the front passenger seat and slamming the car door shut. This car ride was going to be hell, may as well get on with it. Besides, the University had only given me 48 hours to get off campus and not a fiber in my body wanted to stay here a minute longer. I felt a roil in my stomach at the impending questions and texts from my friends that would no doubt be hurtling my way soon. I'd probably even get kicked out of my sorority, not that I cared about that stuff nearly as much as I had freshman year. Too much had happened since then.

My mother slid in the driver's seat and let out a heavy sigh before turning to face me. "Meredith, I know...I know I've been hard on you and I know I'm not always the sweet, supportive mother. But it's because I love you. I really do love you, you know that?" Tears sprang at the corners of her eyes and I immediately missed the anger. My mother and I had a tumultuous relationship. Anger was easier to deal with. Genuine feelings of regret and disappointment? Yeah, that was pure torture.

"I know, Mom. I know that you love me." She nodded once in response and put the car in reverse, driving more slowly than I'm sure she drove on her way here. After a few painful minutes of heavy silence, she finally spoke again.

"I called your father." Her voice was quiet, formal. I whipped my head from staring out the window.

"You what? Why?" I had barely seen or talked to my father over the last eight years. My parents divorced when I was seven. For a few years I shuffled between houses until my dad up and left me to move to Boston. It was like he wanted to wash himself free of me. I'd never been the type to hang onto something that didn't want to hang onto me. Call it pride I guess. Between a birthday card and a call on Christmas, I considered him a stranger. I didn't even know that he and my mom still talked.

"Honey, I'm out of ideas. I've given you every-thing....clothes, trips, tuition to a great University. Maybe you just need a change of scenery or something. Ellis sent her daughter, Amelia, you remember her? From high school? Well her mother sent her to live with her father and it was good for her."

"You just don't want me home with you and Martin for the next four months. It's fair, really. But just call it like it is, Mom. I don't mind." I leveled with her. My tone wasn't angry, it was monotone. Martin and I had never taken to each other. He probably viewed me as the only thing on his cons list when it came to marrying my mother. We avoided each other and that worked for us just fine. There was no way he'd want me back at the breakfast counter after I'd already successfully left the house.

"Meredith, don't talk badly about Martin. That man has saved this family." I rolled my eyes at her response but didn't let her see. "I actually called your Dad a few weeks ago. When you kept getting in trouble for your outfits and for disrupting class. *That* I thought I could still handle. But drugs? Your father has dealt with more in his life than me. He's more...equipped for these types of issues." There was a sourness to her tone, dripping with judgement. Like she was still blaming my dad for behavior that happened over fifteen years ago. All I knew about him was that he was some sort of boxing coach. Maybe boxing and drugs went hand in hand. I didn't care. I'd never tell anyone about what had happened, least of all my estranged father.

I stared out the window for several long minutes, watching the blur of trees along the highway. The sense that this wasn't a discussion but rather a proclamation settled over the interior of the car like dust after a storm. It was done. No use in wasting my energy on trying to convince my mom otherwise. I didn't have the fight left in me.

"I'm assuming there's no point in me disagreeing with this?" I turned to my mom, my arms crossed over my chest. I could feel a heat in my cheeks but I wouldn't let the tears fall. I clenched my teeth tight, physically trapping my emotion.

"I'm afraid not, Meredith. If you're going to hate doing it for you, then consider it a favor for me. For your mother who has been worried sick about you. I never had to worry about my sweet Meredith before! You're supposed to go through this kind of phase in high school, not as a young adult starting your life. I won't tolerate it." My mother's steely veneer was back in place, our brief heart-to-heart from earlier in the drive effectively over.

"Guess I'm going to Boston then." I pulled my earpods from my purse and closed my eyes, my attempt at tuning out the rest of this ride and my current, shithole of a reality.

"Nico! This is too heavy, can you help me?" My littlest sister, Maria, called out to me from behind the bed of my old pickup truck. We were moving out of our shitty temporary housing apartment and into a real, way safer apartment closer to the gym. The fighting tournament contract I'd signed came with an advance. I'd never had so much money in my bank account before. It gave me an entirely new sense of peace at night, especially for my sisters. Getting them out of the shithole we'd grown up in had always been my biggest goal. If my two fists were going to grant us that opportunity, then I'd sure as hell fight anyone or anything to get there.

"Here, you take this." I took the big box from my sister and handed her an armful of towels so she'd still feel useful. We didn't have much shit so the move wouldn't take long.

"Celeste, get the clothes from the back. I need to be back at the gym in an hour." My sixteen year-old sister was already balancing a box of kitchen supplies and a lamp in her arms. She rolled her eyes at me.

"Nico, you're always at the freaking gym. What more can you learn?"

I laughed at that. Most people had no idea how much skill and technique went into what looked like violent brawling on the surface. "More than I have time to learn." I kicked open our new apartment door with my boot and set the heavy box down. The space was airy with two bedrooms and two bathrooms, giving us plenty of room for a change. My throat constricted with the usual sense of responsibility and fear that I felt. If I didn't perform well, we'd lose this place. The advance was generous but it'd only go so far. The constant weight over my head made it hard to enjoy anything for too long, the fear of losing it always winning out. I run my hand over my hair, trying to push down the negative thoughts.

"Hey, lazy bones, there's still a few more items you can grab before you head out." Celeste came up behind me, setting her box in the kitchen and unloading plates and pans. I headed back down the steps, and reached the truck when I saw a girl leaning against the driver's side door.

"Hey, you moving in?" She had long dark hair and tan skin. She nodded up at the open door of our apartment, visible from the parking lot.

"Uh, yeah. I'm Nico." I wiped my hand on my jeans and offered it to her. She took it in hers and gave me a seductive look. Damn, this girl was forward.

"I'm Aria. I live on the second floor. Maybe we should hangout sometime." She cocked her head in a flirty way and I felt a smirk tug at my lips. I was no stranger to attention from women, but it was always casual for me. Caring for two younger sisters I never had enough space in my life for anyone else longterm.

"Yeah, that'd be fun. Let me give you my number--"

"Nico! Hurry it up!" Celeste yelled down at me from outside our door and I shot her back an angry glare. *Yep, that was why I never had serious girlfriends.* I already had two girls in my life and that was more than enough. I looked back at Aria who had a confused look on her face as she looked between Celeste and me. Even though Celeste was only sixteen, she'd already inherited my mother's trademark good looks. I really wish she would've stayed the dorky kid I still pictured her as in my head. Would've made shit a hell of a lot easier.

"Sister." I interjected Aria's thinking to avoid any confusion. "Sixteen and annoying as hell." She giggled at my comment and I moved in a little closer. "Give me your phone."

"Nico!" Celeste yelled out again, clearly just being a pain in the ass on purpose at this point.

"Chill, Celeste!" I took Aria's phone in my hand and quickly programmed my number before pulling a final box out of the truck. I didn't miss the way her eyes went to my arms appreciatively. Fighting definitely had its perks outside the ring.

"So, I'll see you around?" She pushed herself off of my truck, sauntering away.

"Sure." I shifted the box in my arms, making my way back up the stairs.

"About time." Celeste looked back at me sassily as she worked to hang clothes in a hallway closet.

"The first time you bring a guy home? I'm going to make up for all the times you've done shit like that to me."

"Oooo you said a bad word!" My little sister Maria came out of the bedroom, her favorite blanket draped over her shoulders like a cape.

"Sorry, Maria." I ruffled her hair and turned back to

Celeste. "Can you manage dinner? I might be at the gym late tonight since I took this morning off for the move."

"Yeah, no problem." Celeste gave me a look as if to say she wanted a truce. I grabbed my gym bag and headed for the door.

"Hey, Nico?" Celeste called out my name and I turned around, my hand on the doorframe. "This place...it's really nice. Thanks." I could hear all the unspoken words in her voice, the appreciation for what being able to live in a place like this really meant. For all the shit we didn't want to voice out loud in front of eight-year-old Maria.

"I like it too."

## NICO

"**A**nother lap, Nico!" Rhett yelled out at me and I nodded once before upping my pace for another lap. Any of the other fighters would have been rolling their eyes at Rhett making me run extra laps for being late like a kid in middle school, but I didn't care. I always had so much energy, like it was trapped so deep within me that a good portion of it could never get out. The closest I'd get to feeling truly spent was in the ring. The combination of skill, stamina, adrenaline, and pain was the only way for enough energy to leave my body. Otherwise, I was vibrating constantly, quietly manic but still manic nonetheless. One of my foster moms had called me out for it before but no one ever took enough time to really treat it. Fighting had been my choice of therapy.

"Hey, enough running," Coach Barry approached the ring, rubbing his hand over his bald head, "Nico already told me he'd be late. Moved into a new apartment." I came to a stop in front of Coach, catching my breath but not the least bit tired out.

"Yeah, whatever. No excuses." Rhett's tone was teasing

and he threw me a smirk before nodding his head at the ring. "Hop in." We started to go through a few combinations, the movements finally feeling like second nature instead of something to study. All of the motions were now fluid between my jaw and my torso and my fist. When you're first learning the combinations it's like each piece is sequential and different, but as you drill them into your memory there's no way to separate how one part of you moves from another. There's an art to the violence.

"Coach, you look like you just saw a fucking ghost." Rhett looked away from me, keeping the boxing pads up in front of his chest as I pummeled into them one after another. I paused for a moment to look over at Coach Barry and agreed that he did look a little pale. But old white dudes always looked pale compared to a half-hispanic, Olive-skinned guy like me.

"Yeah, well," Coach sighed heavily and leaned his fore-arms on the ropes, "I feel like I'm about to see a ghost. Meredith flies in today. I gotta leave in thirty minutes to pick her up from the airport. I probably won't be back in the gym tonight."

"Who's Meredith?" I kept my fists moving fluidly as I asked my question. I really didn't know shit about Coach other than his legendary training status and that he lives, eats, and breathes this gym.

"My daughter." Coach Barry let out a high-pitched chuckle and it was clearly a mix of despondent humor and nerves.

"I didn't know you had a kid."

"Yeah, well, her mom and I split when she was little and she's been living out in California her whole life, so I wouldn't really say I've been around much. Not winning a 'dad of the year' award anytime soon." He smiled but his expression didn't meet his eyes. Rhett just stood like a statue, sustaining my blows as if he did this shit in his sleep. Hell, the guy probably did dream about fighting. But even I could make out a line of concern for Coach etched across Rhett's brow. Coach Barry wasn't usually the nervous type. Annoyed and ornery, maybe. But nervous? Not a good look for a boxing coach.

"Hey, I'm sure it'll be fine." I turned around quickly and kicked behind me at the boxing pads Rhett was holding, knocking him slightly off balance. Thankfully the faceguard hid my cocky smirk. Rhett wouldn't like that shit one bit. "Plus, if you need any girl advice, I have two younger sisters who are both huge pains in the ass. I may have a survival tip or two."

Coach Barry laughed and pushed himself off the ropes. "I appreciate that, Nico. Always good to have a man around that understands women."

"What about me?" Rhett held up the boxing pads as if to say, *what the fuck*, and Coach Barry just laughed.

"Yeah, definitely no. How Ava puts up with you, is a total mystery." Rhett squinted his eyes at Coach's response and I took the opportunity to move in quickly, getting a few blows to Rhett's abdomen before he managed to roughly grip my shoulders and get me back at an arm's distance. The feeling of getting a few punches in on him was wild.

"Woah there, junior. Save it for the tournament, alright?" Rhett slapped the side of my faceguard jokingly and I gave my patented nod of agreement. But beneath the grill of the faceguard, I was grinning like a wild man, my eyes dancing with electricity. This tournament couldn't come soon enough. Everything in my body told me I was ready.

## MEREDITH

This isn't happening. This isn't happening. I desperately repeated this lame mantra to myself as the airplane cabin's electronic ping indicated that it was time to leave the plane. I looked outside the airplane window and crinkle my nose at the dreary, overcast weather. Gloomy Boston. Definitely not sunny, southern California. At least I wouldn't have to worry about my fair skin getting sunburned. That's about where my list of positives ended.

I head to baggage claim to pick up my suitcase. My palms felt clammy with nerves as I fished my cell phone from my purse and dialed my dad's number. My heart was pounding in my chest at the anxiety of it just being the two of us. I mean, he'd always been a good dad when he was present. I had a few good memories from my youth. But after he moved to Boston over ten years ago, it was like he'd become a stranger. Just sort of slipped through my fingers without much of a fight. I felt myself fidgeting in place as the carousel continued to circle with various black and navy blue bags. *How did no one ever pick up the wrong bag?*

My dad picked up on the second ring. "Hey, Dad." I didn't know what else to say so I just let the silence hang suspended for a moment, hoping he would pick it up.

"Hi, Mer." His voice sounded almost as nervous as mine. Neither of us said anything for another long moment and I rolled my eyes in desperation. *Was it going to be this freaking awkward for the next four months?*

"Just waiting for my suitcase at baggage claim. I'm near terminal C." I eyed my suitcase and moved closer to the carousel, hoping to snag it before someone else mistook it for their identical looking black roller bag.

"Okay, I'll be outside to pick you." He sounded like he was going to hang up but quickly added, "Dark gray truck, Ford." I nodded to myself. Of course I didn't know what car my dad drives. I didn't know any of those little facts about him. Like his favorite food or his favorite movie. Fuck, what if he has a woman living with him? I felt a flush creep into my cheeks and I couldn't believe I hadn't considered this possibility before. My mother didn't mention anything to me about my dad ever moving on, but then again when she did mention him it was usually grumbling about something that happened over twenty years ago.

I rolled my suitcase to the exit doors and felt the gust of cold air hit my overheated face. It was the first, and probably only, time I was grateful for the cooler weather. I saw a massive dark grey truck and a middle aged-man leaning up against the passenger side door. He raised his hand in the most man-type wave I've ever seen and then pulled his jacket tighter around him. *Yep, he's just as uncomfortable as I am.* Not sure if that was reassuring or not.

"You're bald?" I rolled my suitcase up next to the truck and couldn't keep the words from popping out of my mouth. I hadn't seen many pictures of my dad over the years but as a kid, I remembered him having dark red hair like mine. Now, he was bald as a baby.

"Yeah, I'm afraid so," my dad laughed and rubbed his hand over his head before moving in to give me a brief but tight hug. He looked healthy, strong. The bald thing wasn't even a bad look for him, just caught me by surprise.

"Looks good." I gave him an awkward nod before throwing my duffle in the back of his truck while my dad put my suitcase in the bed of the truck.

"You look, wow, you look like a prettier version of your mother." My dad smiled at me and I squinted my eyes.

"Is that a compliment to me or just a dig at mom?"

"Neither. Or maybe both." He shoved his hands in his pockets, a smirk pulling at his mouth. "C'mon, let's get out of here so we can get you some dinner."

The rain falls against the car softly as we head out of the airport and onto the highway. I sent my mom a text to let her know that I landed safely and then power off my phone. The barrage of texts from my friends and classmates had already started coming in over the past two days. I couldn't handle it right now. Maybe never.

"So..." my dad tapped his large knuckles against the truck's steering wheel, glancing between the road and me, "what's new? Other than you getting into some kind of trouble at school from what your mother tells me?"

"I don't want to talk about it." Yeah, fat chance. I just landed five minutes ago and have barely seen you for the last ten years. Not interested in a heart-to-heart.

"Fair, enough. We don't have to talk about that. Just, I mean, if there was anything else you want to talk about."

I glanced up at his profile. He had the same strong jaw and straight nose that I remembered. His skin was pale like mine. Without his dark red hair, we really didn't look much alike. I got my facial features mainly from my mother. But his tone sounded genuine and calm, completely unlike my mother's. I believed him when he said we don't have to talk about *it*. I was grateful for that.

"Well, not much. I'm really just trying to figure out what I'm going to do for the next four months." He glanced over at me and scanned me up and down. It was like I was some strange woman in his car instead of his daughter. We both felt the sense of distance but didn't acknowledge it.

"Well, I think it might be good if you get a job. Doesn't have to be full-time or anything, but work is good for the mind."

"A college dropout in a city where I know no one? Not exactly a great job application."

"You're not a dropout, you're suspended," my dad gave me a serious look with a hint of playfulness in it, "besides, aren't all those super successful billionaire tech gurus college dropouts?"

I rolled my eyes at him. "Yeah but I'm not a tech guru, dad."

"Not yet." He turned his attention back to the road, his fingers drumming louder against the steering wheel.

"Maybe I can get a job as a waitress or something." I didn't want to have to think too hard. Working with my hands, doing repetitive tasks, that could be good for me.

"You know, I have this awesome office manager, Ava, at the gym and she could probably use some --"

"I'm not working at a boxing gym, dad." I cut him off and he just nodded curtly without saying anything else. It's not that I was trying to be a brat, but I still didn't understand this whole boxing and fighting world that my dad was into. My mother painted a really ugly picture of the whole scene and even though I could disagree with my mother on pretty much everything, the idea of a career in violence made my stomach lurch. Well either that, or the fact that it had always felt like my dad left me for his love of boxing. Either way, I wanted nothing to do with it.

We finished the drive in silence. A few minutes after pulling off the highway, my dad was steering through a nice, quiet looking neighborhood. The homes looked way different than in California, far more vertical and narrow. But each house and yard looked well-maintained. It wasn't fancy like where my mom lived with my step dad, Martin, but it was definitely nicer than I had expected.

"Here we are." He pulled into the driveway of a two-story white house. The lawn was perfectly manicured and a large garage was detached from the house, clearly a later add-on. There was a wrap-around porch with an old-school charm but everything looked like it had been repainted and cleaned up.

"This is nice." I hopped out of the truck and pulled my duffle bag from the backseat while my dad got my suitcase.

"You sound surprised."

"Mom kinda painted you as a deadbeat." I regretted the words the minute they left my mouth but was relieved when I heard my dad chuckle.

"That woman never liked me, I swear to god."

We headed inside the house and it smelled good, like chicken and rosemary. I hadn't even realized how hungry I was. My nerves and anxiety over the last few days had kept me from eating much.

"Smells good." I looked around the house, feeling like I'd accidentally broken into a stranger's home.

"Thanks." I jumped at hearing a deep, raw voice and turned to see a huge, tattooed man in my dad's kitchen, leaning up against the counter.

"What the --"

"Meredith, this is Rhett. He used to be my top fighter. Now he's a co-owner at the gym."

"And head coach." The scary but insanely hot man apparently named Rhett, added to my dad's statement.

"Yeah, yeah." My dad waved him off before removing his jacket and setting a few plates on the table.

"You didn't tell me your daughter was a woman." Rhett looked me up and down but his gaze was only clinical, assessing. There wasn't a trace of lust in his eyes. Hopefully the fear and confusion in my expression was covering up how hot I thought he was. I dated cute frat boys in college but this Rhett was...something very, very manly.

"Yeah, well, I didn't quite expect it either. It's been a long time." He looked between Rhett and me and I swear, I wished the kitchen floor would just cave in and swallow me whole. Although, it was true that I must look completely different to my dad. I wasn't a gangly, young redhead anymore. I was a little taller than average at five-foot-seven and had slender curves. I'd been an athlete all my life and kept myself toned and fit. My dark red hair was way past my shoulders, down the middle of my back. My mother always begged me to cut it, but I liked it that way.

"They're gonna call her Ariel." Rhett placed a perfectly golden chicken on the table before he returned to the kitchen to get something else. And even though his huge back and threatening shoulders both scared and excited the shit out of me, I was sick of being talked about in the third person.

"I'm right here. And who are they?" My dad looked up at me with a tired but kind look on his face.

"Sorry, Mer," he cleared his throat and took a drink from

his water glass, motioning for me to sit down at the table, "he's talking about the men at the gym."

"I'm not going to the gym." I looked up at Rhett as he brought over a steaming bowl of fettuccine, and despite my edge of frustration I heard my stomach growl.

"Don't be shy, eat." Rhett winked at me and despite my mouth popping open at his forwardness I didn't have my usual snappy comeback prepared. Instead, I shoveled a heaping mound of pasta and chicken breast onto my plate. *Damn this guy could cook! Who would've thought.*

"I have your bedroom made up for you," my dad cut into his chicken, looking at me nervously, "I always had a room for you but was never sure how you'd like it decorated. I had Ava, Rhett's girl, help me out with it. But you can change whatever or let me know if you need anything else."

I swallowed past the lump in my throat to get the mouthful of fettuccine I'd just taken down. Something in my dad's tone told me that he'd thought about me a lot. More than I'd imagined. I'd always kind of figured he'd been happy to be rid of us. Not that he was evil or anything, just that the family-man life hadn't been for him. But the way he talked about my bedroom made it sound like he'd really missed me.

"Thanks. I'm sure it'll be great." I finished my dinner in silence and Rhett got up after wolfing down nearly half the chicken.

"Gonna go pick up Ava from Shelly's place. See you at the gym tomorrow." He headed toward the hallway, turning back once to look over his shoulder, "Go easy on him, Meredith." He winked again and I blushed despite thinking he was kind of an ass. *How could a woman not?*

"Don't even think about it." I whipped my head up at my

dad, surprised by his tone. It wasn't menacing but there's a strong protectiveness to it. Something I wasn't used to.

"I'm not."

"You were."

"Was not."

"Fine." My dad picked up our empty plates and loaded them in the dishwasher. "Upstairs and to the right, let me know if you need anything." I nodded and stood up from the table. The stairs were just off the hallway from the kitchen and all the banister work looked like it had been restored. There was something charming about the house that made it feel cozy, more like a home. I headed up to my new room, thinking these next four months might not be quite as hellish as I had originally figured. Well, as long as I kept my phone off and myself away from the boxing gym anyway.

The sweat dripped into my eyes but I didn't even need my vision. I could *feel* what I needed to do next. *Jab-jab-cross. Duck and defend. Jab-cross-hook-cross. Uppercut to the left.* I got Rhett off balance just long enough to jab him hard in his side, holding nothing back. He faltered and I moved in closer, pummeling his ribs before I heard him yell out to stop.

"Alright, alright. Jesus, Nico, no one fights during training as viciously as you. Not even me." Rhett's chest dand I looked him square in the eye. He gave me a nod without saying anything else. For me, it was all the recognition that I needed. The former king of the underground was telling me I was ready to go after my own crown.

"Fuck, Rhett! Get over here!" I heard Coach Barry yell out, and while the dude always seemed to be yelling at us in the ring there was a sense of urgency in his voice. Rhett looked at me and shrugged before hopping swiftly out of the ring and I quickly followed suit after him.

"What's going on?" I leaned over Coach as he held the head of one of the newest fighters between his hands.

"I didn't mean to hit him that hard, Coach, I promise." Another new recruit looked on nervously. The fighter being held by Coach glanced frighteningly around him like an animal that was trapped and couldn't move.

"It's okay, son. Part of the sport. We all know this when we enter the ring." Coach slowly slid a head cast looking thing around the fallen fighter and immobilized his head completely.

"Nico, go get my phone, it's in my office. I want to make sure we get my favorite doc. I only trust my boys with the best." I nodded at Coach Barry and sprinted off to his office, my limbs still firing with the energy of the ring and the urgency of the situation. Broken ribs, bloody noses, gashed eyes. Those injuries I was used to. Even a broken arm wouldn't stop me in a fight. But a neck injury? The possibility of being paralyzed? Fucking shit. Having good technique in the ring was about far more than just winning. It was about saving your goddamn life. I had to keep that in mind every time I stepped into the ring. Even in practice. My sisters needed me.

I grabbed Coach Barry's cell phone off his desk. As I headed back toward him, he put the fighter on a stretcher and talked to a few medics. The other young fighter looked like he was about to puke. Coach's phone started vibrating and I glanced down. I saw the name "Meredith" flash across the screen.

"Yo, Coach, some chick named Meredith is calling you." I tried not to get in his way as he managed the chaos of the medical situation, standing slightly behind the group.

"Meredith? Give me the phone." I handed it to him, not knowing if I should leave or stick around.

"You what? Oh man, what are the chances." Coach rubbed his hand over his head, looking stressed between the stretcher carrying out one of his newest recruits and the medical crew. "Let me, uh..." Coach glanced around, a conflicted look on his face, "we're having a bit of a situation at the gym...I think I can get home in about an hour or two, that work?" He nodded and said a few more short phrases before hanging up. I turned around to find Rhett and see if he wanted to keep training me for the afternoon or if we were all calling it a day.

"Nico! Wait up." Coach's voice was out of breath as he jogged over to me. "I hate to ask you to do this, but I need a favor. I gotta head to the hospital to make sure they treat Duncan right. First priority is to get him healthy, but the second is to get him back in the ring. Don't want any impatient doctors making shortcuts that could hinder that." He gave me a tight smile and I nodded in response. "My daughter, Meredith, she uh...well she picked up the wrong damn suitcase at the airport yesterday. Honestly, I can't blame her. I've always wondered how that doesn't happen more often. Anyway, she basically has no stuff without her suitcase and I could be at the hospital for hours based on the look of Duncan's neck. You think you could swing by my place and take her to the airport? You've got sisters, I can trust you with this." Coach looked desperate, almost pleading. It wasn't a style I'd seen from him before. This man and Rhett had taken me in. Given me a shot at a real, fucking career. Changed my life for my sisters and me. Driving his daughter to the airport so she could get the proper suitcase? Hell yeah, I could do that. I'd driven Celeste to the fucking hair salon before, and then back again when she wouldn't stop crying about the haircut they gave her. So yeah, dealing with Coach's daughter for a few hours was the least I could do.

"Sure thing, Coach. No problem." He smiled at me gratefully and then his expression hardened.

"I *can* trust you, Nico, right?"

"Yeah, Coach. I promise." I knew Coach Barry had dealt with his fair share of brawling, trouble-making, law-breaking fighters so I couldn't blame him for being concerned. But I just wasn't that type. I wasn't looking to be *bad*. I had been dealt *bad*. And trouble wasn't something sexy or exciting that you sought out when it had been lurking around every corner ever since you were a kid. It was something to run *from*, and fucking fast. Good thing I was fast as hell.

"Okay, yeah, you're a good one. One of the good guys as they say. I'll text you the address. Head home after. Gym sessions are closed for the rest of today."

"You got it." I headed over to the locker room to grab my gym back and plugged the texted address from Coach into my phone. I also saw a reminder ping from my calendar. Only a few weeks left until I left for my tournament. After today's injury, I'd be more mindful stepping into that ring, but never less excited. I loved that feeling more than anything, and I couldn't wait to share that with a real, live audience.

## 8

## MEREDITH

I literally jinxed myself. When I opened the black suitcase this morning, I was greeted with a few, nearly identical-looking men's suits. Yeah, definitely not my luggage. My duffle bag really only contained my personal items, so unless I wanted to wear the same outfit everyday for the next four months, or invest in an entirely new wardrobe, I'd need to get my proper suitcase back. And also give back a bunch of suits to some stressed out, traveling businessman.

My dad sounded completely stressed when I called him. Of course, I'm one day in and I already fucked something up. I considered telling my mother but I didn't. Honestly, the worst part of the whole thing was having to turn my cell phone back on. The device was practically overheating in my hand, vibrating and pinging itself to death. I responded to a few messages from my closest friends but left everything as vague as possible. I swore I'd never say anything about what happened, even if keeping a secret to protect *him* killed me inside. If I told anyone why I'd gotten into so much trouble over the past few months, the only person it would come back to bite in the ass would be me. No thank you.

I glanced down as another text came through my phone but thankfully this time it was just from my dad.

DAD @ 10:30 AM: Sorry Mer, looks like I'm going to be held up for a few hours longer. I sent someone from the gym to drive you to the airport. Text me when you're back home. -Dad.

MY STOMACH FLIPPED. *Fuck, what if he sends that Rhett guy?* He was intimidating as hell. An entire forty-minutes alone with him in the car? I think I'd combust from nerves alone. Before I could send a reply to my dad, I heard the loud engine of a truck outside. I headed down the stairs and peered out the front window, seeing a large, old truck in my dad's driveway. The front passenger doors popped open and a tall, olive-skinned guy leapt out with the agility of a jungle cat. I felt my jaw literally pop open and I thanked my lucky stars that I was alone and hopefully well hidden from my current vantage point in the window. He started walking toward the front door, his dark hair slicked back like he just ran or took a shower, hard to say which. His arms and legs were long and lean but muscular, each muscle rippling as he moved. He was wearing a pair of gray joggers and a tight-fitting black t-shirt. I couldn't quite see his face as he ducked his head and neared the door. I nervously scooted back from the window, not wanting to look like a total freaking creep. Couldn't I go one day here without encountering an uncomfortably attractive man?

I heard a quick knocking at the front door, and

smoothed down my hair. My heart was pounding in my chest but I didn't let it show on my face. My go-to reaction these days when I was nervous or uncomfortable was just to be an apathetic brat. Call it survival instinct after what had happened. Regardless, I was no longer a fan of showing much emotion. Men would just exploit that shit, especially the good-looking ones. I squared my shoulders and fixed my features into the perfect mixture of sass and apathy before unlocking the door.

"Who are you?" I propped my hip against the door frame, keeping my gaze steady. *Holy shit.* His jaw was perfectly cut and his eyes were a honey brown against his tan skin. He was an uncommon mixture of pretty boy meets rough around the edges and it was totally disarming me on the inside. Like, who the hell is this guy and how does my dad know him?

"Uh, hey..." He shoved his hands in the pockets of his jockers and looked behind my head as if he was expecting someone else to be in the house. "Are you the babysitter? Or..."

"The babysitter? What are you talking about?"

"For Coach Barry's daughter, Meredith. He sent me to take her to the airport to pick up the right bag or something."

"I'm Meredith. Meredith Barry." My tone was practically caustic. His gorgeous eyes went wide and a smile pulled at his lips but he didn't let himself give into it fully. I swear I saw a dimple appear but at this point I could just be imagining things.

"Oh, shit." He rubbed his hand along his jaw, unknowingly showing off a set of rippling veins in his forearm. "I'm really fucking sorry. You're, like, way older than I thought."

I couldn't help the huff that escaped me. Geez, did the

stress of this year add wrinkles to my face or something? I felt heat creep into my cheeks and I internally cursed at how annoyingly easily I flush. "I look old? Thanks. Nice to meet you too." I head out the door, closing it forcefully behind me and locking it with the key my dad had left me this morning.

"No, no, not in a bad way," He started walking after me as I headed toward his truck, "I just thought you were like thirteen, that's all."

"Yeah, well, I'm not." I gave him a sarcastic smile and hopped up into the cab of his truck, which was not an easy feat. The thing was a beast.

## 9

# NICO

H*oly freaking shit.* Coach Barry's daughter was a total dime. Like really jaw-dropping gorgeous. The kind of pretty that made me goddamn uncomfortable. I'm not sure I've ever seen a girl with hair the color of hers. It's a really dark red, and falls long around her shoulders. How did Coach, with his bald head and beady eyes, create a human like *this?* She was hot as hell but also seemed cold as ice. When I told Coach that I understood women, I was talking about the younger sister variety. The madder than hell sexy redhead next to me? Yeah, I had no idea how to deal with this chick.

I hopped up into the cab of the truck with Meredith already in the passenger seat. She had her arms crossed and was staring straight ahead. Damn, this was going to be a long two hours. I slowly reversed out of Coach's driveway, looking back to see that she'd already thrown the black suitcase in the backseat.

"Have you ever done that before?" I nodded at the suitcase, trying to make conversation and break the silence.

When she turned her head to me, I felt my palms get sweaty against the wheel. This girl was way too fucking pretty. It was startling. I was good around women, fairly smooth when my sisters weren't getting in the way, but I wasn't much of a player. I was pretty much a straight shooter and didn't engage in games. Never really went for girls way out of my league and just stuck to my own. This girl had me fidgeting in my seat.

"No." She flipped her hair sassily and looked at me like I just asked the dumbest question on the planet. *Nice work, Nico.* The guys at the gym would have my balls if they could see how big of an idiot I'd made of myself in the last several minutes. I decided to keep my mouth shut and opt for the radio, turning up the volume loud enough to combat the awkwardness. It didn't help much. Finally Meredith broke the silence.

"So, how do you know my dad? From the gym?" She kept her gaze bored but there was a small fierceness and curiosity in her expression alongside it.

"He's my coach. Well, and Rhett too. Rhett's my mentor." I saw her expression shift, a genuine look of surprise that she didn't manage to cover up.

"Rhett's your mentor? You're a fighter, or whatever?"

"Uh...yeah. You sound surprised. I don't look like a fighter to you?"

"Not really. You're...I don't know. You're just not beefy enough." I let out a chuckle at her comment and flashed her a quick smile before focusing my attention back on the road. I was definitely one of the leanest guys at the gym, looking more like an athlete than some barrel-chested backroom brawler. Rhett was similar, but he was an inch or two shorter than me and rougher around the edges, his muscles formed into hard, impenetrable knots whereas mine were more languid like a soccer player's. It was my biggest asset, ironically, even if it meant I didn't fit the fighter build stereotype.

"Do you know a lot about fighting?" I looked over at her and noticed that she was studying me but trying to appear like she wasn't.

"Other than the fact that it's bloody and violent? No, I don't know much else," she kicked her feet up onto my dash and looked out the passenger window, "not interested either."

I nodded but she couldn't see me so it was really just a nod to myself. I always nod. Always agree. I'm never looking to be difficult, just looking to work hard and catch a break. If this hot chick wasn't into fighting or fighters, I'm sure as hell the last person that could convince her otherwise. Besides, I'm just here trying to do good by my Coach. As gorgeous as this sassy redhead is, there's no way I'd touch her with a ten foot pole. That would be seven different shades of trouble, all of which I didn't need. *Just three weeks out. Three weeks until you're on the road, fighting for real.*

"You can just loop around, I'll take the suitcase in." Meredith looked out the window at the airport dropoff zone.

"I can come in with you, I don't mind." I switched into the park lane and Meredith didn't say anything so I figured she wouldn't bite my head off but it was hard to tell with this one. I parked the truck and pulled her bag out of the back before she could get to it. I noticed a snarky look on her pretty face but she pursed her lips and headed toward the terminal with me behind, towing her bag. Coach would have my ass if I didn't act like a helpful gentleman or whatever.

We entered the bustling airport near the baggage claim

and headed over to a help desk. When the cold AC of the airport hit me, it was the first time I realized that I was still fully sweaty from the gym, barely having thrown on a pair of sweats and t-shirt before hopping in my truck and heading to Coach's address. Meredith was probably used to clean-cut frat boys instead of a half-latino, high school dropout. She looked about college-aged, a few years younger than me.

"Hi, I picked up the wrong bag when I flew in yesterday. From LAX." She tapped her fingers on the help-desk counter and the pieces started to click in place. *California girl.* Clearly here in Boston with her dad against her will. I hadn't known Coach Barry for longer than a year but the only time I'd ever heard him mention that he had a kid was when he found out she was coming to stay with him. Not exactly the signs of a friendly visit.

"Ah, yes, we had a return yesterday evening as well." The woman behind the counter gave Meredith a tight smile before her eyes caught mine. I noticed a faint red blush spread on the attendant's cheeks and she smiled shyly before turning back to her keyboard.

"Really." Meredith squinted her eyes at me, her voice a harsh whisper.

"What?" I threw up my hands innocently, whispering back.

"Boys." She crossed her arms back over her chest and leaned her hip against the counter as the airport employee got up and went through a door behind her desk.

"Look, I don't know what's pissing you off, or how I came to be the cause of it, but I'm not a boy. I'm a man. And I'm just trying to do right by my Coach. Nothing else." My voice was measured but my words held weight. This chick may be prettier than any girl I'd ever seen in real life, but I wouldn't have her lumping me in with whatever fuck boy stereotypes she'd been dealing with lately. I had my sister, Celeste, and her friends to thank for even knowing what a *fuck boy* was.

She opened her mouth like she was about to respond but the attendant returned, interrupting us. "Here's your luggage, Miss Barry. I'll take that other suitcase from you." Meredith tried to lift it over the counter but struggled with the weight. I instinctively reached out and lifted it over the top, earning another flustered smile from Miss Airport Lady. I just nodded curtly and ducked my head, ready to get the hell out of here.

Meredith pulled up the handle of her new suitcase and started wheeling it towards the exit.

"Wait up," I tapped her shoulder lightly to get her attention, "shouldn't you check it first? You know, just in case?" I wasn't even trying to be a dick. The suitcase she was rolling looked the exact same as every other suitcase in this terminal. The chances were probably one in a million that it would happen twice, but I sure as hell wasn't driving her back here if it did. She looked up at me like she wanted to argue, but didn't. Instead she sets the suitcase down on its back and unzipped the sides. She threw back the top cover. Laying on top of her loosely packed clothes was a pale blue lacy thong. She paused awkwardly for a moment before brusquely zipping the suitcase back up.

"Yep, it's mine." She didn't face me but I could see a little red on her cheeks. It was more satisfying than seeing it on the lady behind the airport counter, that's for sure. Probably because Coach's daughter didn't seem like the kind of girl to get embarrassed easily. *God, I have to get the image of her dark red hair and perfect pale skin in that blue lacy thing out of my head, and fast.*

"Cool." We headed back to my truck in silence, and after I helped her get the suitcase in the back we hopped into the cab.

"So," I drummed my hand nervously against the steering wheel, "you're staying with your dad for a while?" Part of me expected her to ignore my question completely, but when I looked over, her face appeared a little softer. Almost like she was letting her guard slip a bit.

"That's the plan. My mother's plan at least." She gave me a sardonic smile. "I got in a little trouble at school and well, here I am." She waved down her body and I couldn't help my eyes from tracking her. She was long and athletic, with feminine, delicate curves. It was fucking *hard* not to notice but I was still trying like hell.

"What are you going to do? While you're here?"

"No freaking clue. But whatever it is, at least I'll have my clothes." She gave me a small smile and it somehow transformed her face. Made her pretty features look way less intimidating and instead more inviting. But it was gone just as quickly and I turned my eyes back to the road.

"I never went to college. Will you go back?" I'm not even sure how much I care, but forty minutes goes a lot faster with a little conversation.

"Probably. What else am I going to do?" Her voice sounded far off like she was thinking about something unsaid. I didn't pry, that's never been my style. Instead, I turned the radio dial up, gently ending the conversation.

"How long have you been fighting at my dad's gym?" I was surprised by her question and turned to face her as I exited off the highway.

"About a year. I fought for a year or two before that, but not with formal training or anything. I was basically signing myself up to get my ass kicked," I laughed a little at the memory, my flailing wild arms and unending energy making me a fun bet for the crowd, but I'd taken more than my fair share of beatings, "but then your dad and Rhett recruited me and now I'm about to enter my first legit tournament." The excitement of the upcoming tournament flooded through me again. I'd barely talked about it with anyone, not that I really had that many people to talk to about it. My sisters hated talking about the stuff and most of my friends at this point were other fighters at the gym.

"What do you mean by legit tournament? There are illegitimate tournaments, like illegal stuff?" Her eyes went wide and I rubbed my hand across my jaw, trying to figure out how to answer. Clearly this sheltered girl didn't know shit about what her dad was into, and fuck if it was my place to be the one to break the news to her.

"Uh, I mean, just that the tournament I'm entering...it's a big deal. Good money, lots of travel and press. That kind of thing." That wasn't technically a lie. I mean sure, I'd dodged her question about the underground thing, but getting in between family matters was none of my business.

"Are you scared?' Her voice was the most genuine I'd heard since I picked her up. I pulled my truck into Coach's driveway, idling slowly to a stop before putting it in park. I threw my arm over the back of my seat and turned my body to face her.

"Nah, not really. I'm pretty fucking excited." I smiled at her but her face was blank in response. We just sat there, like something else should be said but no one really knew what it should be. Then she abruptly threw open the door and hopped out of the cab before pulling her suitcase from the back seat. I tried to get out to help her but she was already halfway to the front door.

"Well, thanks. Sorry my dad made you drive me."

"No problem. He's a great coach."

"Nice to know." She shrugged her slender shoulders before unlocking the front door of the house and heading inside. Coach Barry had a fucking, beautiful handfull on his hands, that was for damn sure.

## 10

## MEREDITH

I flopped down on my bed after putting away some clothes from my suitcase in the small closet in my new bedroom. My mom had always described what my dad did for a living to me like it was some sort of seedy, pathetic world for wash-ups and deadbeats. But Nico was young and vibrant. His energy was almost contagious and the look of pure excitement and passion on his face when I'd asked him whether he was nervous about an upcoming fight stayed with me long after he dropped me off.

My dad probably wouldn't be home for another few hours. Since landing, I'd barely spent any one-on-one time with him other than the airport car ride. I wasn't mad about it. Maybe even a little relieved by it, if I was being completely honest. But tonight would probably be our first sit-down dinner alone. I pulled my phone out from my purse, being sure to keep it in do not disturb mode, and sent Toni a quick text asking if she could talk. My phone started vibrating a few moments later.

"Hey, Red, how have you been?' Toni's voice was filled

with a mixture of awe and concern and it made me want to roll my eyes. She was always theatrical but never dramatic like other girls.

"Don't call me that," I sat up on my bed and leaned back against the headboard.

"How are you holding up?"

"Do people really think it's that bad?"

"Do people think *what* is that bad? Everyone's already well and moved on from the mystery of your semester disappearance." Toni gave out a little snort over the phone and even though she sometimes annoyed the hell out of me, I was grateful for her humorous demeanor.

"Really?"

"Well...no. But who cares. People talk, they love to gossip. It's only been a few days. Give it a few weeks and people really will have moved on."

I groaned at Toni's response, knowing that she was right but still hating the idea of what kinds of things people must be saying about me. "What are the biggest rumors?" My curiosity always got the best of me. Hell, it was the foundation for why I was in this mess in the first place.

"Meredith..." Toni's voice wavered before a heavy sigh let me know that she was going to acquiesce to my question, "Well definitely that you're pregnant. That's a big one. Also that you're sick with a crazy, incurable virus, but that's not nearly as exciting. And," she paused for a second before continuing, "that you had an affair with one of the professors."

My eyes popped out of my head at her words and it made me want to laugh hysterically. My only male professor was a small, greyish man with a frog-like face and beady little eyes. Mr. Helmose. Definitely not happening.

"Is...is it true?" Toni's voice left her in a whoosh like the wind just got knocked out of her chest.

"What? That I'm pregnant with my professor's baby?" I laughed before continuing, "Not even a little bit. No judgement but Mr. Helmose is not my type, and hell I'm probably not his either." Toni laughed at my response but didn't say anything else. I could feel her sharp mind working in overdrive. I'd known this girl since middle school.

"I'm not pregnant with anyone else's baby or sick either, Toni."

"Then, what is it? You know that you can tell me and I won't tell anyone. I'd never do that to you."

"I know." And I really did know. Toni had always been a way better friend to me than I deserved and she could be trusted more than anyone. "It's just...I don't want to talk about it yet. I don't think it will really help. It's over. I did what I had to do."

"What do you mean, what you had to do?"

"Toni...look, all I'm saying is that I got involved in some shit and it's done. There's nothing else to worry about." I was saying the words as much for her as for myself.

"Fine, but you know that if you ever want to--"

"I know."

"Okay, good. So, how's your old man? Is it weird after all these years?"

I rolled over onto my stomach, grateful for the change in conversation. "Yeah, it's super weird. I really don't even know him yet, but his life isn't really anything like my mom described it. He is some fighting or boxing coach, I don't really know, and has all these weirdly attractive fighters working for him."

"Woah, what? This is way more interesting than your pregnancy rumors," Toni laughed, "What's the gym like?

Are there just a million punching bags everywhere like in the movies? Or is it like Fight Club where you can't tell me about it?"

"I don't know, I haven't been. I wasn't planning on going. You know how the sight of blood makes me want to pass out."

"Meredith, you have to go check it out. My older brother goes to those, like, sanctioned matches or whatever. They sometimes have them an hour away from campus. It's basically like a concert, but sweatier. People get really into it." Her comment brought Nico back to my mind. The tall, muscular olive-skinned force of energy. He was a strange mix between the single-minded focus of a boy with the determination of a man. I could picture him under stage lights, his chest rising and falling after he beat his opponent...what would it be like to see someone like him doing that live? I felt a line of energy flow from the back of my neck to my hips and I stood up to pace in the bedroom.

"Maybe..."

"Maybe my ass! Look, if you're not going to be in school for the next four months, you may as well live a little. Just go check it out. If it's some gross, sweaty basement with fugly creeps then just leave." I laughed out loud at her comment, knowing damn-well that neither Rhett nor Nico fit that description *at all.*

"Thanks, Toni."

"For what?"

"For, I don't know, just always being there."

"You're going soft on me, Red. Call me after you check out the gym. I'll be eagerly awaiting updates." Toni hung up and I smiled to myself, her quirkiness uplifting my spirits a little.

Maybe I should go check out the gym. I mean, it was my

dad's whole life after all and it seemed pretty damn near impossible to get to know him without the context of that place. What's the worst that could happen? Not to mention there might be a chance I'd see Nico again in his element.

## 11

## NICO

"Hey, Celeste!" I yelled from the kitchen to be heard over her blaring pop music, "Come here for a sec, we need to talk." I'd be leaving in a few short weeks, and it would be the first time I'd really left my sisters' side. I knew Celeste could handle it. Despite her annoying behavior whenever I was talking to girls, she was definitely mature for her age. And Maria was still young enough to be an angel and not yet a pre-teen demon. But I still had my concerns, and the weight of the responsibility I felt for these two never lessened even as we got older.

I left the dirty dishes in the sink and sat down at the table, shredding a napkin between my fingers. Old nervous habit.

"What's up?" Celeste plopped down, her phone still in her hand like it was permanently attached to her body.

"We need to talk about when I leave. I will be able to fly home a few times throughout the year, but I'll pretty much be on the road most of the time." She nodded and her face perked up at the level of seriousness in my voice.

"I know..."

"I just...you're only sixteen. I mean, it's not ideal to leave you and Maria here alone."

"Nico, we've been through way worse. And this place," she gestured her hands to the kitchen, "is so much safer and nicer than where we used to live. It will be fine, I promise." She looked down at the table and then up at me. "You've done enough...so much for us. I can take care of Maria and me for a little while. You can't worry about this kind of shit when you're fighting."

"Language, Celeste."

"Seriously, Nico?"

I sighed and scrubbed my hand down my face. Celeste was right. In order to make the most of this opportunity and really give myself the best chance in the ring, all of my focus had to be centered on my stance and my strength and my fists. Not on whether or not Celeste and Maria were managing well enough on their own. Still, way easier said than done.

"I'll be able to transfer money to you every two weeks, for whatever you two need."

"It. Will. Be. Fine. Hermano." Celeste got up from her chair and kissed my forehead before taking her phone back into her bedroom. I started back on the dishes when I heard my phone ringing. It was Coach Barry.

"Hey, Coach." I propped the phone between my ear and my shoulder, scrubbing spaghetti sauce off of Maria's plate.

"Nico, hey. Look, I'm headed home from the hospital and I just wanted to call and thank you again for helping out my Meredith. I hate to ask you to do errands like that for me, but I was just in a tight spot."

"Sure thing, Coach. No problem." *No problem my ass.* That sexy redhead was one hell of a conundrum. But I sure as shit couldn't say that to Coach. I'd thought about her off and on throughout the afternoon. She wasn't easy to forget.

"Well, you get some rest. I'm sure Rhett will be looking to kick your ass tomorrow in the gym since today's session was cut short."

I smiled at his words, "Wouldn't expect anything less."

## 12

## MEREDITH

"Let's head out in five, okay?" I heard my dad yell from downstairs and I glanced nervously between my reflection in the mirror and my open bedroom door. It had been my idea, after all, to ask my dad if I could come with him to see the gym. Well, I guess technically it had been Toni's bright idea, but now I was starting to regret the decision. I didn't know what to wear to a fighting, training gym. I mean who would even know that? It's not like I'd be slipping on a pair of silk shorts and boxing gloves and making my way into a ring or anything. I spun around one more time, resigned to be content with my favorite pair of faded denim jeans and a short-sleeved knit shirt. I opted for sneakers since even I knew wearing heels to a gym was stupid.

I threw on my favorite LA Dodgers baseball hat and grabbed my purse before heading downstairs.

"How do you like your coffee?" My dad was wearing a pair of gray sweatpants and a long-sleeved t-shirt. He had a steaming pot of coffee poised over two to-go cups.

"Black. Thanks." I ran my hands down my arms and grabbed one of my dad's sweatshirts from the coat rack.

"Me too." He gave me a small smile. It wasn't not much but it was something in common.

We headed to his truck and I was grateful for the sweatshirt as the cool air nipped at the back of my neck. California weather had definitely spoiled me. I took a grateful gulp of hot coffee, the liquid warming me throughout.

"So, I hope I'm not going to be in the way or anything," I took another sip of coffee and glanced furtively over at my dad.

"Oh not at all, honey. I actually really want you to meet Ava. She's our office manager and I think you'll really like her." He turned the heat up in the car and I felt my cheeks start to flush from the warmth.

"Okay cool," I paused before continuing, "I don't...I don't, like, want to work there or anything. I just wanted to check it out. Learn more about...what you do." I tried to soften the sting of my earlier words and kept my voice bright. But I didn't want my dad getting any ideas. Earlier he'd mentioned me working at the gym. Going on a sight-seeing mission so that I could call Toni and tell her about it was not the same as working full-time for a violent enterprise. Besides, I couldn't imagine being less qualified to work at a freaking boxing gym.

"All good," my dad smiled, but I could see a hint of tightness around his eyes. God this was awkward. Always one step forward, two steps back. At least he wasn't the yelling type like my mom.

We pulled up to the gym and parked in a designated spot in front. The building looked like a huge, renovated warehouse with darkly stained concrete walls and large industrial windows covered in an opaque film that only let light in. The front doors were on industrial rollers and my dad pulled at the large steel handle to get them moving. I heard the gym before I saw it. Deep, bass-heavy music flowed throughout, mixed with the sounds of leather being hit and weights being dropped. I heard a few bursts of laughter, punctured with a string of curses. *Geez, I thought my mouth was bad.* But there was definitely something undeniably cool about it. The gym was clean and huge, giving plenty of space between different sparring rings, weight sets, and punching bags. There was a floating loft in one corner with a metal staircase leading up to it and a partially exposed office table. I tried to sneakily snap a few photos without looking like a total loser. Toni would appreciate the visual evidence.

"Hey, Coach!" I heard a deep, gravelly yell and turned to see Rhett approaching us. His eyes raked over me, in that same mechanical cool way they did in my dad's kitchen. No desire, just awareness. And annoyance. I didn't know if this was just Rhett's morning face, but he did not look happy to see us.

"Coach..." His voice trailed but he didn't say anything else. He sounded like a petulant child which was hard to imagine considering this man seemed like he was *never* a child. Like he was just born a fully-fledged, tattooed adult.

"She's my daughter, Rhett." My dad's voice was low and I whipped my head quickly between the two of them, not understanding why the heck their secret conversation had anything to do with me. Rhett just nodded and placed his hands on his hips, avoiding glancing again in my direction.

"Ava will be in the office in an hour. We need to start booking Nico's flights. The kid is ready as hell. He needs a little ring time to work out some...energy." Rhett's thick eyebrows raised on his forehead and I could tell there were more unspoken words taking place. I shifted awkwardly in my sneakers, reflexively pulling my cap down lower over my face as if that would somehow make me disappear.

"Yeah, he's ready. I want Meredith to meet Ava when she comes in. Meredith," my dad finally turned to me as if he just remembered I'd been standing beside him the whole time, "why don't you take a look around and meet me in the office up those stairs in half an hour?" I nodded quickly and gave him a closed-lip smile before scuttling off toward the punching bags with my coffee in hand. Anything to get away from the palpable tension between my dad and Rhett.

I heard a rhythmic thud that was getting increasingly faster. It was like the beat of a drum underwater, steady but also undulating at the same time. I peaked around another row of bags, feeling like a little kid in a maze. I was greeted by a long, lean back, every muscle rippling and re-settling in exact alignment with the sound of the speed bag. Small rivulets of sweat traveled down from where dark wavy dark hair met a strong sweaty neck to the tops of a pair of workout shorts. I felt like a total stalker but I couldn't turn my eyes away, the movement of his body hypnotic...

"Oh, shit!" The speed bag suddenly stopped as my stainless steel coffee cup hit the floor. The sound of it crashing to the ground ceased the melodic sound of the leather. I scrambled to the floor, luckily righting the cup before too much coffee spilled out. *Why do these damn travel mugs have to sound like a gong just went off when they hit the floor?* When I stood up, Nico was staring at me. An empty but bright expression on his handsome face. He had one hand on the speed bag, his rest rising and falling as he caught his breath.

"Meredith?" He grabbed a towel near him and wiped it down his face roughly. *Why did that have to be so hot for no reason?*

"Uh, yeah. Hey. Sorry to interrupt, I, um, just came with my dad for the day. To, you know, check out the place where he spends all his time." I gave him a weak smile and could feel my patented blush spreading over my cheeks. I pulled my baseball cap down a little lower.

"How's your suitcase?"

"My what?"

"Your suitcase...the one we picked up from the airport. I mean, how is it having your clothes back?" Nico faltered on his last sentence, now the one in the awkward seat. I was all the more happy to give it to him.

"It's great. Wearing some of them right now." My tone defaulted to slightly bitchy, which always happened when I felt shy or nervous. *Add it to my list of things to work on.* Nico just nodded and then his brow furrowed deeply, like he had something else more meaningful he wanted to say.

"Sorry, I didn't mean to interrupt you," I gestured between Nico and the speed bag and started to make my way out of the leather maze, "I'll see ya around." I ducked my head quickly and headed to the other side of the gym, suddenly finding weight racks so incredibly interesting that I had to get near them at once. I didn't know if I'd ever really had *game* with guys other than them thinking I was pretty, but there was something about the combination of Nico's hotness and his eagerness...like he was so honest and pure but also simultaneously training to punch other grown men in the mouth and break their ribs...that had me totally and completely flustered around him. Good thing I wouldn't be coming back here much.

## 13

---

## NICO

*hit.* Why did Coach's daughter have to throw me off so much? Celeste would be dying laughing if she could have witnessed how lame I had been just now. But to be fair, Meredith wasn't much smoother either. The girl just set me on edge. It wasn't even because she was beautiful. There was something else, something more. It was like she herself was agitated and annoyed with the world, making me feel like I did something to piss her off while having absolutely no clue what it could be. The last thing I needed was my Coach's daughter putting a bug in his ear that I was some sort of loser. I walked over a few feet to a large, worn punching bag and hit hard, the force radiating into my elbow and up through my shoulder.

One punch became two, became ten. I wasn't even focusing on technique or my breathing. I was just releasing. Women like Meredith knocked my confidence and painfully reminded me that I'd never be good enough, educated enough, rich enough for an entire part of the world to care about me. I didn't even seek out those things in life but I was still desperate for acceptance and for competence. How could I ever get out from under the pressure of proving myself and my sisters worthy when all we'd ever been was looked down on? I channeled the anger into the bag, driving relentlessly until I heard a high-pitched cat-call whistle and drop my arms.

"Damn, Nico," one of the fighters, Bevy, came up beside me and leaned against the bag. He was a small but compact guy, his muscles dense and overlapping like they never quite stretched out properly. He reminded me more of a wrestler than a boxer but the guy could takedown men twice his size.

"What?" I reached for a towel, drenching it in sweat.

"You see that fine as hell redhead walking through here? I ain't never seen hair like that before, man. God, I'd love to wrap it around my wrist and take her from—"

"Coach's daughter." My voice was hoarse and I saw his pale eyebrows stitch together in confusion as I grabbed a water bottle next to the bag station.

"What?" His voice was incredulous.

"She's Coach's daughter." I didn't need to say, *don't even think about it.* That shit was more than implied, and in addition to Meredith making me feel like an awkward piece of shit, I'd been having to remind myself of the same mantra more than once.

"No way..." Bevy's tone and expression took on a far-off look as he glanced over at Coach's office.

"Yep." I tried to sound as if I didn't care. I mean, why should I? She was gorgeous and I'm not the only man who's going to notice. But looks only went so far. Something about Meredith was not at all pretty on the inside.

"That is a fucking shame, man. She may as well be radioactive. Or a dude." I chuckled lightly at his comment but resolved to push the topic out of my mind. I couldn't imagine her wanting to spend much time around the gym anyway. Plus, I'd be on the road soon. The thought brought a more positive energy to me.

"I gotta go talk to Ava about my tour schedule. Keep your dirty thoughts to yourself."

"Ah, shit. Why'd you have to say 'Ava' and 'dirty' together?"

"Bevy, I'm pretty sure talking about Rhett's girl could get your ass beat even more than Coach's daughter."

"You wagering a bet?" Bevy started to bound on his toes in excitement. The dude was a consummate gambler, betting on his own odds in the underground which was a huge 'hell no' even in that lawless world.

"No." I turned from him and started to head in the direction of Coach's office, a fresh towel draped over my shoulders.

## 14

---

## MEREDITH

After my awkward encounter with Nico, I made my way through a quick tour of the rest of the expansive gym and up into the safety of my dad's loft office. Could I have looked anymore like a creep, staring at his back as he pummeled that little mini punching bag thing? Was that what they called a speed bag? I wanted to groan at the thought but I forced it out of my mind. Clearly Nico had felt just as awkward as me after I interrupted his workout, trying desperately to make conversation about my luggage. God, my life had well and truly imploded.

"Meredith?" I turned at the sound of a sweet, eager voice and saw a really pretty brunette smiling at me, her arms loaded down with papers.

"Hi, here let me help you." I grabbed some of the forms from her arms. They looked like some type of legal contract or purchase orders.

"I'm Ava. It's so nice to finally meet you!" She took a seat across from me and the warmth in her smile made it hard not to smile back.

"You're the office manager, right?" I recall my dad

mentioning Ava as the office manager and also as Rhett's girlfriend. Lucky lady.

"Indeed." Her smile became more gentle like she was reflecting on something from her past, "I never thought I'd work in a fighting gym, but here we are! I love it. We've been busier than ever with all the new fighters over the past year."

"How did you," I swallowed, trying to find the right words without coming across as rude which was frustratingly not an easy task for me, "uh, find this place?"

Ava let out a little laugh and started to form the papers into separate piles. "I wasn't looking for it, that's for sure. I was studying marketing in college. I'd always planned on moving to New York and working at a big, fancy consultancy. Maybe on fashion accounts." She looked at me giddily like two old friends sharing a secret. She couldn't have been more than a few years older than me. "But then my dad got into some serious trouble. White collar trouble. And basically, my whole world fell apart. I moved in with my best friend Shelly and she was dating a fighter, Eric. If you see a huge curly-headed beast down on the floor, that's him." She paused for a moment but I didn't interject, intrigued by her story. "Shelly dragged me to the gym with Eric and to my first underground fight. I was so against it. I mean, blood and me? Heck no. But slowly, this world and I fell in love. There's a lot more to it. The fighters, they...they have so much self-discipline and strength that goes beyond the physical. It's like an art. Violent but still art. And then there's all the coordination that goes into it. Hours training, special diets, sleep routines, equipment requests, contract negotiations, PR for the official fighters...the list goes on. That's the kind of stuff I like, so I just stuck around."

"And Rhett?" The words popped out of my mouth of

their own volition. But Ava didn't seem to mind. She smiled kindly and ran her hand through her hair.

"Well, he's at the center of it all for me. But, we're a team. It's always best that way." I nodded at her vague response, wanting to fully understand what she meant but having no real reference. I'd had boyfriends. I'd dated. But the most serious guy that had come into my life had just about ruined it. Not sure I'd ever be brave enough to try that again.

"What are these piles?" I cleared my throat to change the topic. Ava seemed like the kind of person you could actually open up to, even after only knowing her for a few minutes. But I wasn't the opening-up kind.

"Oh, Nico's contracts are in this pile right here." She laughed, a faint look of stress covering her face, "Everyone wants him. Since signing up for the X League Fighting series, I have new PR and appearance requests weekly. That kid is a star...I mean, I really shouldn't call him a kid. I think he's my age. But something about him is just, I don't know, more pure than the rest." She glanced at me quickly and I kept my face as expressionless as possible. Hearing someone else talk about Nico was strangely alluring. I wanted to know more, to ask questions. *How old was he exactly? Why did Ava sense that same energy and vitality that I had? What's his backstory?* But before I could even consider asking, Ava had already moved onto the next pile.

"These are equipment purchase orders. These guys train so hard, they literally break *everything*. When I first got a job here, I thought the fighters went through an obscene number of towels. But, turns out they just go through an obscene number of everything. And this last pile is one-pagers for new applicants. We used to just recruit guys like Nico and Rhett. Fighters from the underground with prom- ise. But now that the gym's training program has grown so much, we have some pretty fancy applicants wanting to get in." She smiled up at me before turning to a desk drawer and pulling out a pen.

"So," I tapped my knuckles lightly on the top of the desk, "are Rhett and Nico like...really good? At fighting?" My curiosity got the best of me and I couldn't help but pry a little. At the least, I could convince myself I was just getting entertaining intel for Toni.

"Rhett was the best. I'm not just saying that because I'm in love with him," her lips pulled up at the corners, "he really was. But he fought like every fight might kill him. Totally threw his body into it every time, no matter the physical cost. He's got some pretty serious injuries. But he won the underground, beat every other top-ranked fighter in that scene." Ava set her pen down and leaned forward just slightly, her voice lowered a touch.

"But Rhett thinks Nico is better. He'd never admit that within the four walls of this gym, but he knows it. Nico's athleticism and energy...his ability to bounce back and stay light. I don't know what it is exactly, but the way Rhett describes it is that it's rare. Nico could really go all the way."

I felt a warmth in my cheeks, my thoughts betraying me slightly. I rushed to cover them up. "Damn, that's crazy. I always just associated fighting with, like, Hulk Hogan or whatever." Ava laughed heartily and I joined in with her, glad that she wasn't the least bit offended.

"To be fair, I guess at one point I probably did too."

"Hey, ladies," My dad entered the office, his face slightly shiny, "how are Nico's travel plans coming? His first flight should be in ten days or so, right?"

Ava's face shifted from humorous to stressed, "Yes, but I'm still having a hard time securing the tour manager. The person we want won't be available for another six months.

He's doing a circuit in Europe. I can help Nico with his first two fights, but after that--"

"Rhett will want you back here," my dad finished her sentence.

"I mean, this gym is my baby at this point," Ava chided him, "I want to be back here too."

"I know," my dad sat down in his desk chair with a heavy sigh, closing his eyelids briefly, "we'll have to figure something out. I can't travel every week and Rhett sure as shit hates being on the road too much if he's not the one fighting. Do we have any other candidates?"

As my dad and Ava went back and forth on office business, I pulled out my phone to send Toni a few pictures of the gym that I surreptitiously took this morning. But just after I hit send, my stomach dropped and my heart started to race in my throat at the text message I saw flash across my screen:

HEWITT @ 10:15 AM: You can't ignore me forever. We need to meet. Face to face.

I GLANCED UP, squirming in my seat. I suddenly got the urge to pound one of those huge leather bags downstairs. Either that or sprint a mile in the cool air outside. I tried to take in slow, even breaths through my nose but it was not easy with the adrenaline coursing through me.

"We just need to find someone that can be a tour manager for four or five months. Someone who is organized and isn't opposed to being in a different city every week." Ava started chewing on the tip of her black pen, her mind clearly working.

"I'll do it." My voice was slightly breathless and I sat up straighter in my chair.

"What?" My dad turned to face me, his palm flat on his bald head.

"I'll do it. I'll be the tour manager or whatever. Until I go back to school." The words flew from my mouth in choppy spurts. I didn't know what I was agreeing to. I only knew why. I needed to be on the move. Hewitt would find me if I stayed in one place. He was relentless. And I'd do anything to avoid that.

"Well," my dad chuckled lightly but the sound held a tone of concern, "let's chat over dinner and we can sleep on it. How about that?" Ava nodded at him and looked excitedly between us, having found a solution to her problem. *Hopefully, I'd found one too.*

## 15

## MEREDITH

I pushed my broccoli around my plate. I was actually one of those weird people that really liked broccoli, but my stomach felt like it had been somersaulting ever since receiving that text from Hewitt. I never responded and he didn't text again. He didn't need to. Hewitt had a lot of shitty qualities, but he always followed through on his word. Which would end up being rather unfortunate for me.

My dad looked between my plate and me and let out a deep sigh, "You'll have to ask your mother. I mean, I don't mind you doing it. I trust Ava to help you prep and I think the travel and responsibility would be a great experience. But..." He ran his hand over his bald head.

"But what?"

"On these tours, there's a lot of...riff raff. And not the college-kid stuff. I'm talking hard drugs and prostitutes, among other things. I don't know if that kind of environment is safe for you right now and--"

"Dad," I cut him off, dropping my fork loudly, "I'm not an addict or anything. I got involved with the wrong group. I was in the wrong place at the wrong time...too many times. But I don't have any interest or desire in doing drugs at all," I swallowed past a painful lump in my throat, "trust me. Please." He studied my face for a long moment and I wanted to look away, but I held his gaze. My dad didn't know me inside and out like my mother did. I'd need him to trust me on these words alone. I still wasn't' ready to talk about what had happened, but I knew I'd never touch drugs again. And I wouldn't be tempted by that stuff on Nico's tour. I needed this job. I had no idea if I'd do it well, or how I'd manage to not make an awkward and bitchy fool out of myself around Nico every waking minute, but when you're desperate you take what you can get. And this could be my lifeline for the next four months.

"I believe you, Meredith. I do. But you still have to ask your mother. I'll tell her that I support it, and I'll do what I can to convince her. But she raised you all these years. I can't just send you off without having her blessing." I hated that what my dad said made sense. It was the truth. I stood up from the table, quickly rinsing my plate in the sink.

"I'm going to call her now," I slipped out of the kitchen and up the stairs to my bedroom. My phone felt like a lead weight in my hand and my finger hovered over the "Mom" contact button. We hadn't spoken much since I'd gotten to Boston. It was better that way. Our conversations these days usually ended in a blistering blow-up resulting in me being shipped across the country.

"Hi, mom," I tried to keep my tone cheery but not suspicious.

"Sweetheart! How are you doing? I know you still hate me for sending you off like that. Has your father been feeding you? I swear that man doesn't even know how to make a frozen pizza." I tilted my head curiously at her words, noting the fact that not only was my dad a decent cook, but Rhett had practically been a world-class chef. But I didn't think now would be the best time to bring any of that up though.

"I've been fine. The fridge is stocked. I uh," I cleared my throat slightly, "I actually wanted to ask you about something. I got offered a job for the next few months and...I want to take it. I think it will be good for me."

I could feel my mom's pause before she answered, "Well, sweetie, I mean a job is fantastic. I've always told you how you have to be building your resume *before* you graduate if you want a shot at one of the more competitive firms..." I rolled my eyes as my mom droned on about the importance of having a twenty page resume before I even turned twenty-two. Finally, she stopped lecturing and asked me about the job.

"Well, it's a manager position. A tour manager for a...performer," I chose my words selectively, making the last minute decision to not mention that the performer was actually an alarmingly hot man with an apparent innate ability to knock other men's teeth in. "I'll be traveling over the next four months, helping with events and PR and fan appearances..." *Again, technically all true.*

"Meredith, this sounds very exciting!" I could hear my mother's mental wheels spinning. "Who is the performer? My friends are going to be so impressed when they hear about this. Does your dad know you've been offered this job?"

I wanted to choke on the irony but I calmed myself. One question at a time. "Well, the thing is, I don't actually know who the performer is yet. The management team reached out to me and I have to sign a bunch of NDA's before I actually get to meet them. Apparently they are pretty high profile," the lies spilled from my mouth with ease, "And yeah, dad knows. He's totally cool with it. I'd be back in Boston every few weeks." I took a deep breath and continued to pace the carpet of my bedroom, hoping my mom would buy the story.

"Well, as long as there's no trouble, Meredith. I know these high profile celebrities and performers can get mixed up in all sorts of mischief. Elizabeth Elby, Mariah's mom from your summer camp, do you remember her? Anyway, she used to know that lead actress on--"

"Mom," I couldn't keep the exasperation from my voice, "it will be fine. I promise. I've learned my lesson and I'm not interested in any trouble. I just want to work for the next four months and do something useful during this time instead of laying around all day alone."

"I knew it would be tough for you at your father's," my mother's automatic go-to always being a criticism of my dad even though I hadn't even mentioned anything about him being the issue. "I want weekly phone calls and updates. No ghosting on me as the kids say." I wanted to groan at my mother's request but I trapped it in. I could do a weekly phone call if it meant being on the road and far away from where anyone expected me. Especially Hewitt.

"Deal, mom."

## 16

## NICO

The hot stream of shower water down my back felt good after a long day of sweat followed by an ice bath. Something about the stark contrast in temperatures always made my worn muscles feel good. I stepped out of the shower and scrubbed my hair with one of the gym towels, then wrapped it around my waist.

"Hey, pretty boy! Coach Barry wants to see you," I heard Bevy yell at me from the locker room entrance.

"Okay, I'll be out in ten!" I shouted back and made quick work of drying off my body before slipping on a pair of jeans and a black t-shirt. A few of us from the gym were heading out for drinks tonight and I'd texted the Aria girl from my apartment complex to see if she'd want to join. I had turned down a few of her dinner requests, knowing I'd be on the road soon and not wanting to be that guy who leads a girl on for a few weeks before literally taking off for the next year. Still, I was looking forward to letting off some steam tonight and enjoying one of my last nights out in the city.

I packed up my gym bag and slung it over my shoulder.

The locker room exit was near Coach's office loft and I made quick work of the stairs, two at a time. I rapped my knuckles on the half-exposed wall by way of greeting to see if it was cool for me to enter.

"Nico, come on in," Coach's voice rang out and I rounded the wall to enter his office. My limbs went stiff at seeing Meredith sitting next to him, her dark red hair falling around her shoulders and a nervous expression on her beautiful face. She broke eye contact with me quickly, gently toying with a stack of contracts in front of her like they were suddenly the most interesting things in the world.

"Take a seat, Nico," Coach's voice was light and whatever good mood he was in didn't seem to be translating to Meredith. I sat down cautiously but showed no emotion on my face.

"What's up, Coach?"

"Well, Nico, we have some good news," at the mention of 'we' Avacame into the office and took a seat on the other side of Coach, her usual bright smile on her face, "we've found you an interim tour manager." I glanced between Coach and Ava, feeling myself relax at the topic of conversation. I knew this had been a stressful point for Ava since her top pick was off in Europe or something and wouldn't be available for another few months.

"That's awesome, who is it?" I ran my fingers through my wet hair, trying to tame the wayward strands that always got extra crazy as it dried.

"Meredith!" Coach smiled brightly at me before turning to face his daughter. Her face was stone, barely moving, but she forced out a tight smile when seeing her dad's proud face. She barely looked at me, keeping her gaze a few inches down and focused on the table.

I knew I had to say something. I should've *already* said

something. But I couldn't speak. I'd only had a handful of small interactions with this chick and they hadn't been great. I was awkward as hell around her, warring between not liking her attitude and finding her irresistibly attractive yet totally unattainable in only about a million ways. I didn't even know if I liked her. Let alone, the thought of spending nearly every waking minute of my dream fighting tour with her by my side? I wanted to pull a Rhett and say 'no.' Flatout pull a fucking diva move and demand that it be somebody else. Anybody else. But how could I? This was my Coach's freaking daughter. I snapped my head in surprise when it was finally Mereidth who broke the awkward silence.

"I'm really looking forward to it, Nico." Her voice was robotic, professional. I felt my eyes go wide and it was like Meredith and I were having our own, secret conversation. Basically me saying "what the fuck is this really about" and her not answering.

"She's going to be great, Nico," Ava clapped her hands together, "we've been going over flight schedules and PR checklists. She's got a razor sharp memory," Ava winked at Meredith who managed to smile back, a little more genuinely this time.

"Well, that's about it, son. Feel free to head out. Your first flight is already on the books. Tour kicks off in Phoenix." Coach Barry stood up from his desk and put out his hand. For a moment I didn't know what he wanted me to do until I realized he was looking for a handshake. He grasped my hand in his, somehow feeling like we were making two very different deals right now. I gave my signature nod before slipping out of the office and down the flight of steps. *Fuck I didn't need this.* Meredith would distract my focus, keep me on edge. I considered venting to Rhett and seeking his advice, but decided against it. His relationship with Coach Barry was too strong.

"Yo, you ready to get shitfaced tonight?" Bevy came up and slapped me on the back, reeking of too-strong cologne. Normally I'd tell him to piss off and that I didn't drink on the weekdays but right now, a stiff one sounded exactly like what I needed.

"Hell yeah. Let's get out of here."

## 17

## MEREDITH

My stomach felt like I was on a ship out at sea. The look on Nico's face when he'd found out that I'd be his tour manager for a few months was *not* good. It wasn't angry. That wasn't a look that seemed to manifest on Nico's handsome face too often. But it was definitely a mixture of shock and dread. Did he not think I was competent enough to do the job? I mean, I know that I'd been shipped off to live with my father because I'd fucked up royally in college, but before that I'd been a straight A student and I knew I could handle the demands of the job, especially with Ava's guidance.

"Are we ready to go?" Shelly bounded out into her small and overly decorated living room where I was sitting awkwardly on the couch. I used to love going out and getting ready with the girls, but I barely knew these two. Ava was super sweet and easy to get along with, but Shelly was feisty and unpredictable. I stood up from the couch and smoothed my palms down my jeans.

"Where are we going?" I took another sip from my pregrame vodka lemonade and admired Ava's hair as she ran her fingers through it, loosening the soft barrel curls.

"A bar near the gym, Pietro's I think," Shelly waved her hand absently in my direction before applying a final layer of makeup.

"So will, like, all the fighters be there?" I shifted from foot to foot, pulling out my phone to text Toni so I could have someone to talk to throughout the night in case this turned out to be awkward as hell.

"Yes! But other guys too, in case fighters aren't your type. I could see that being not your thing considering your dad is a coach and all," Shelly threw me a friendly smile and then glanced over me like she was assessing me for the first time. "Your hair is seriously insane, Meredith. Like I almost don't believe it's real. Is it?" I let out a polite laugh, but it was a question I'd heard throughout my life and grown used to.

"All real, as far as I know," I finished off my drink and placed it on the counter with a thud. Tonight would be the first night that I'd be drinking in a while. The last time I'd gotten drunk had been with Hewitt, and well that night had been the beginning of the end...

"You look great, Meredith. Tonight will be fun, I promise." Ava gave me a small side hug and grabbed her purse before we made our way downstairs to the Uber. The thought of seeing Nico made a fresh wave of nerves course throughout my body. Maybe I'd have an opportunity to confront him and figure out what his problem was. Get it all out on the table and over with before our first flight next week. I *needed* this job more than he could really understand, so I'd have to put my nerves aside, suck up my pride, and set this shit straight.

The bar was noisy, but thankfully not so loud that you had to yell just to hear the person next to you. There was a well-lit outdoor area with heaters and breezeways that led into the inside of the bar. The place was far from new, but it had a charm that appealed to me, almost like a few of the college bars back in California. I fell in step behind Shelly and Ava, letting them lead the way to the bar.

"Hi, baby." Ava leaned up on her toes, even in boots, and kissed Rhett. The contrast between the two of them was extreme. Ava, all soft and feminine and sweet and Rhett hardened on literally every surface. But it was clear that they were so in sync with one another. Even when Hewitt and I had been good, it was never anything like *that*. I pulled my eyes away and ordered a vodka soda at the bar, casually scanning in search of Nico's tall shoulders and olive skin. If I saw him in a bar, I'd never know that he was a fighter. Athlete, for sure, but seeing some of these other boxers around the bar and at the tables on the patio, Nico didn't even seem like he was from the same planet. There was something cat-like and elegant about him, mixed with power and agility. I tried to keep my thoughts professional, noting the fact that the better Nico was in the ring, the longer my tour managing duties would last, but I couldn't deny the traitorous pink flush that crawled up my neck at the thought of his strength, thankfully hidden by the darkness of the evening.

"Hey," a friendly voice came up behind me, and a short, stalky fighter was smiling brightly at me. He looked nice somehow, harmless even, despite the bulging of his neck and biceps.

"Hi." I took another sip of my drink, not giving away much.

"You're Coach's daughter, right? Cali girl." He smiled even wider on the last words and I couldn't help but offer him a humored small smile back.

"Yep, that's me. But I usually go by Meredith. Coach's daughter just doesn't quite roll off the tongue." He laughed at my comment, his square-like head thrown back a little on his thick neck.

"I'm Bevy."

"That's your real name?" I turned toward him, genuinely intrigued.

"Yep. At least that's what my mom told me." We both laughed until I stopped abruptly as Nico sidled up behind him, leaning one long forearm on the bar.

"Hey, Nico." I stood up straighter, thankful for the two vodka drinks already coursing through my system. I wasn't going to let this opportunity pass.

"Hey," His face was blank and hard to read, but his eyes looked almost worried. Maybe suspicious.

"Nico, can we, uh, talk for a few minutes? About the upcoming travel details?" My voice was a bit too forceful but if I didn't get it out now, then I probably wouldn't get it out at all.

Bevy grabbed his fresh beer from the wooden bartop and took a step backward, "I'll take that as my queue." I almost wished he would've stayed, but I guess it was better just the two of us.

"So," I cleared my throat, "why don't you want me to be your tour manager? No bullshit." I crossed my arms over my chest, my face fixing into a cold but aloof expression. My bitch mode kicked in, the one I seemed to fall right into whenever I was uncomfortable or nervous. Nico didn't respond right away, his mouth opening once and then closing.

"What makes you think that?"

## 18

---

## NICO

I felt like a frog was in my throat. I hadn't even expected to see Meredith at this bar tonight and I definitely hadn't expected her to hit me with a question like *that*. I was also about four drinks deep, which wasn't a normal thing for me these days, so her pretty red hair and determined face were starting to blur together as I dragged my fingers up and down the wet condensation of my drink's glass. There was no way that I'd admit outright how she made me uncomfortable as hell with whatever chip was on her shoulder, not to mention she was distractingly beautiful despite the huge neon flashing "off-limits" sign that could practically be seen over her head as Coach Barry's daughter.

"Well, for starters, you looked pretty shocked when my dad gave you the news. And not in a good way." She slid around to a bar stool and perched atop it, clearly indicating this wasn't going to be a two second conversation. *Great, I should've stopped at drink number two.*

"Uh, well, you know..." My train of thought was fuzzy, "I was just genuinely surprised, that's all. You didn't seem like you were into all the fighting stuff." I shrugged innocently but her expression revealed nothing. There was a long pause before she spoke again.

"Are you drunk?" She squinted her green eyes at me and placed one palm flat on the bartop.

"Uh, well, depends on how you define--"

"You're wasted."

"I would definitely not say wasted." I let out an embarrassing scoff and took a healthy pull from my new drink before noting the disapproving look on her face.

"This can't happen." She shook her head, her dark red hair like a fiery cloud around her shoulders.

"Huh?" Her words were far off in the distance, like I was hearing a delayed echo instead of listening to her real time.

"This," she gestured at my chest, "you, getting drunk. Can't happen on the tour." Her tone was clipped and professional.

"Oh, so it's going to be like that?" My lips pulled into a smile and I could see a resoundly stubborn look on her pretty face. I quickly turned away and went back to my drink. This chick had no sense of humor.

"Look," she put her face closer to mine, forcing me to look back at her, "you're right. I'm not into the fighting thing, whatever this all is anyway. But I need this job and I'm good at keeping things organized and on track. So, as long as you can cool it on the gin, I think we will be able to work just fine together for the next few months. Deal?" She stuck out her slender hand and for some reason I felt like we were two little kids, making a deal in a backyard fort instead of talking about a high-stakes boxing tour.

"How'd you know I was drinking gin?"

"You smell like the inside of a Hendricks bottle." She finished the rest of whatever she was drinking and slid off the barstool to stand. "We're good?"

"Mhmm," I ran a hand through my hair, "good." *Had I actually agreed to something?* My head was swimming with alcohol and confusion but there was a professionally satisfied look on Meredith's face which I figured was better than her earlier annoyed and pouty look. The next few months were going to be...interesting to say the least. But if Meredith was all about business, then there'd be nothing to worry about it. And I could keep my focus where it belonged. In the ring.

## 19

# MEREDITH

The flight from Boston to Philadelphia was short and I was eagerly checking the to do list on my iPhone after we landed. I pulled up my email with the hotel confirmation details as the plane taxied and peered over the headrest in front of me in search of Nico's dark, unruly hair. He was several rows ahead on the plane.

We hadn't said much when we met at the gate this morning. The last time we'd been to the airport together had been when my dad asked him to help me fix my mixed-up suitcase. I pretty much just repacked the thing exactly like when I'd left California, wanting everything that I had on me for the next few months while I was on the road. I flushed at the memory of seeing Nico for the first time, his smooth olive skin and disarming good looks not at all what I had pictured when my mom told me past stories of my dad's fighting gym.

When I finally made my way off the plane, Nico was waiting. His long strong body was leaning up against the wall, a lazy and casual demeanor masking the constant vibration of energy and nerves that permeated Nico at all times. I fixed my face into a blank and professional expression, not wanting to reveal that I'd been openly checking him out.

"The car should be picking us up in fifteen and the hotel is only twenty minutes away," I started reciting my notes from memory, determined to keep Nico's schedule squeaky clean and on track. I was actually grateful to have this job for the next four months, needing something to entirely consume my energy and my focus other than worrisome thoughts of my college life and of...Hewitt.

"Uh, cool, thanks," Nico smiled warmly at me like he was unsure of how we should treat each other. He casually started moving toward the airport exit. The silence was awkward, despite the business and noise of various travellers surrounding us.

When we slid into the backseat of the black car that I'd ordered with the help of Ava, I became all too aware of Nico's proximity. His legs were long and strong, barely brushing up against my thigh but I felt the heat spread over my skin.

"The W Hotel on 5th, correct?" The driver connected with my eyes in the rearview mirror, his voice confident and to the point.

"Yes, that's correct. Thank you." He smiled sharply, and turned to face the road.

"A little weekend getaway?" The driver's voice was clear over the low tones of the radio and I shifted awkwardly against the leather.

"Um, no. Business trip." I cringed at how forceful my voice was and turned to face the window. The driver looked back at us in the rearview mirror and seemed to almost shrug as if my response wasn't what he would've guessed but he didn't really care either way.

When we arrived at the hotel, I headed to reception and provided my confirmation number to the Swedish looking woman standing elegantly behind the front desk.

"Hmm," she tapped her long red fingernails on the keyboard, "there seems to have been a slight mixup. You said you booked two rooms, correct?" Her pale blue eyes were scanning the screen and my pulse started to race. This was Nico's first fight, his first leg of the tour. I couldn't actually be having a problem with my planning already, could I?

"Yes, two rooms. One king and one queen. I have the email right here--" I hovered my phone toward her face but she didn't seem too interested. She shook her head slightly and removed her stylish dark rimmed glasses.

"I'm afraid the mistake is on our end. We have you in a suite, with a king sized bed and a pullout sofa. We will certainly discount your room for the mistake."

"But, I--"

"It's fine, thank you," Nico paused for a moment while he read the receptionist's name tag, "Lillian." I could feel the warmth from Nico's body as his long forearm leaned on the counter. I didn't miss the way Lillian smiley shyly. She seemed to have completely forgotten my presence.

"Thank you for your understanding. Again, my sincerest apologies." Nico just flashed her a friendly smile before taking the keycards and grabbing my suitcase along with his own. Before I could say anything, he was already striding off toward the elevator bay and I struggled to catch up.

"Nico, I'm sorry. I really did book two rooms, I double-checked everything and--"

"Meredith, it's all good, you're doing great." He swiped the key and hit the button for the tenth floor.

"Is it that obvious how hard I'm trying?" I scoffed a little, mainly at myself. Despite my recent reputation as a troublemaker, I was type A through and through. And I really didn't like to mess up. I wasn't exactly go-with-the-flow or roll-with-the-punches. Ironically.

"I like people that try hard. Effort is more than half the battle. No shame in that." He gave me a strange look that I couldn't quite place but before I could overthink it, the elevator doors slid open and we started making our way down the elegantly carpeted hallway.

I had my first fight in a matter of hours. I wasn't nervous, I was excited. Thrilled. But right now I was also distracted by the far-too-pretty redhead who was currently obsessing over every detail of my tour. I couldn't really tell what her true intentions were in taking this temporary gig. If she was just someone who likes doing things right or if she was genuinely nervous. There was almost a desperation to her obsession with everything going perfectly and it sent off a warning signal that I decided would be best for me to just ignore.

"You can sleep in the bed, I'll take the couch," Meredith strolled through the suite, analyzing it as if it were a crime scene and not a luxury hotel room.

"We can figure it out later, no worries."

"Another car will be picking you up in an hour to head to the training gym. Are you hungry at all? I think I have your diet schedule somewhere..." She started rifling through her bag and I resisted the urge to interrupt her and let her know that I was starving. "Oh, yep, you need to eat. Like thirty minutes ago. Let me call the chef, apparently there's a great guy here that Rhett has used in the past and I think Ava had him prepare some meals for you." Meredith was completely absorbed in her latest task so I sent a quick text to my sisters, letting them know I landed safely.

"Okay, your lunch will be here in twenty minutes. I'm going to schedule the car that picks you up after the fight and brings you back to the hotel. We have another flight tomorrow but it's not super early..." her eyes flashed to mine briefly before she continued, "Sorry, I know that I'm rambling but I just want to make sure these first few matches go smoothly. Don't want to...you know, let my dad down." I nodded at her remark, somehow not fully believing it, but it did remind me, once again, that this was Coach Barry's daughter. *Why was that reminder starting to sound more like a warning I wanted to ignore?*

Half an hour later, I was scarfing down my protein-packed lunch while Meredith hid behind her computer screen.

"What time will you get to the arena?" I polished off my plate and leaned back in the chair.

"I'm sorry? You'll head from the training gym to the arena around 7:00 PM. They are only five minutes from one another."

"Yeah, but what about you? Did you schedule a car to pick you up from the hotel?" Her pretty green eyes went a little wide as she slowly lowered her laptop screen.

"Um, I'm not going to the arena." Her statement came out more like a question. I wasn't sure how to respond. "Am I supposed to? Do the tour managers have to go to the fights?"

"I don't know if they *have* to go," I cleared my throat, "most tour managers *want* to go."

"Oh."

"Oh?"

"I've, uh, never been. To a fight." She looked nervous and I felt the need to backpedal.

"You don't have to go if you don't want to. Seriously, no big deal." I stood up from the table to start getting ready for my stretching and training session. Meredith pulled up her laptop screen again. It was strange, having her dad as my Coach and her here as my tour manager and yet she'd never even been to a fight. How did she even know what all this work was for, what it was really all about, if she hadn't seen the action in the ring?

## 21

## MEREDITH

It had been several hours since I'd last seen Nico. After he left for the training gym, I worked through some more to-do items from Ava and went over various checklists for our upcoming tour stop locations. But I still couldn't get Nico's words and reaction out of my mind. I mean, on the surface it made total sense. Of course I should go to Nico's fights. He was, in essence, my client after all. But part of me didn't want to go to a fight and I wasn't passionate about this world like other tour managers probably were. This was temporary. A stop gap between me and my real life and more importantly, a way to stay out of any single location for too long. I hadn't received another text from Hewitt since before leaving Boston, but I knew him well. Too well. One would be coming my way soon. The guy was a total control freak and having me AWOL and unreachable was not going to fly with him for much longer. I knew I needed a more long term solution when my current tactic of pure avoidance wore out.

I was still deciding whether or not I should go to the

fight, so I decided to call Toni. Even though I was 99% sure she'd be on team, *go to the freakin fight.*

"Meredith! How's Boston treating you, what's the latest?"

"I'm actually in Philadelphia..."

"Damn, well, you sure didn't last in Boston long. What are you doing there?" I took a deep breath before responding to Toni's question.

"I, uh, I'm kind of working for my dad..."

"Do not tell me you are kickboxing. Because I might freak out, that is so badass!" I couldn't keep from laughing at Toni's insanely ridiculous assumption.

"Toni, I'm pretty sure I cried during every game of dodgeball throughout our childhood PE class. I am not cut out for professional kickboxing or any form of sport whatsoever."

"True. You were kind of a wimp in all competitive sports. Even cross country. So what are you doing for your dad then?"

"I'm kind of a tour manager?" My voice came out high like a question, "for one of his newer fighters. Apparently the guy has a lot of potential or something." I started pacing the kitchen space, glancing at the clothes I'd laid out on the couch, wondering what kind of outfit one wore to a professional fighting match anyway.

"Are. You. Serious. Ohmygod. Meredith, when did this happen? How could you not have told me immediately? Who's the fighter? Is he hot?" Toni's rapid fire questions had me pulling the phone away from the nearness of my ear and placing her on speaker as I poured myself a glass of sparkling water.

"Uh, like two days ago. I was too busy packing. His name is Nico." I took another gulp after responding.

"You didn't answer my last question."

"What?"

"Is he hot?" I glanced around the room at Toni's question, somehow embarrassed even though Nico was miles away from here. Nico was insanely hot. Sexy, strong, energetic. Somehow pure in a way that men who throw deathly punches shouldn't be. But saying all of that would just make me sound like a freak with a crush I didn't have.

"Yeah, I guess he's hot."

"Liar. He must be sex on a stick, I can hear it in your voice." I didn't miss the satisfaction in Toni's words and I rolled my eyes in response. "So, is he really good in the ring? My brother would be so freakin' jealous of you right now. I am too, for the record."

"I mean, that's what they say..."

"You haven't seen him fight yet?"

"Nope."

"Well, when is his first fight?"

"Tonight. That's actually why I called. I really hadn't planned on going but then he seemed surprised and almost offended and now I feel like--"

"GO! Meredith. Non-negotiable. I'm telling you, these matches are really fun. The energy is insane and you will literally be in the best seats. You'd be actually clinically insane not to go."

"I wish you could come with me." Toni made everything more fun, more relaxed. She was a good yin to my yang. But she was also all the way across the country. I'd have to fly solo tonight.

"Uh, duh. You know I'd be there in a heartbeat if the dimensions of time and space weren't very real things." Toni snorted at her own nerdy comment.

"So, what do I wear? I mean, you said it's basically like a concert, right?"

I spent the next hour Facetiming Toni while trying on several different outfits and then variations of the same outfits before we settled on dark black jeans and a form-fitted silky top which I'm pretty sure was what I had planned on wearing before even calling Toni. I had also ordered my favorite spicy margarita to the hotel room to loosen up my nerves a bit. Ever since I'd gone to the Chancellor's office and received the news about my suspension, I hadn't even thought about having any more *fun*. The concept of *fun* had felt as distant as the ocean in the Sahara.

The air outside was chilly and I pulled my coat tighter around me. I'd ordered myself a car through the same service I'd scheduled for Nico. I'd debated texting him to let him know that I had decided to come, but I chose not to bother him. He was busy getting into the right headspace or whatever and my coming to the fight was probably a way bigger deal in my head than it was to anybody else.

As we got closer to the arena, the lights of cars glittered along the road, traffic at a near standstill. I couldn't believe the crowd, and I peered out of the backseat window to try and see how long we'd be waiting in line.

"Hi, sorry to ask, but is there an employee lane? I work for one of the fighters."

"You do?" My driver turned in his seat, bracing one beefy arm over the back of the passenger headrest. His face turned into a half-smirk. "What exactly do you *do* for this fighter?" A sour look covered my face at his innuendo and my eyebrows raised up onto my forehead.

"Tour manager. It's a real job. I have a badge." I pulled out the badge that Ava had put in my travel packet and flashed the driver with it, effectively removing the smirk from his face.

"Okay, yeah, we can go in the fast lane once we get up to

the next turn." He grumbled back at me, seemingly disappointed in my boring and strait-laced story before turning his attention back to face the road.

When I finally made it through VIP security, the match was only half an hour from starting. A tall skinny guy with tattoos lacing around his arms and neck ushered me to my seat. The arena was dimly lit and vibrating with energy. There was a constant drum, a hum, that you could feel in your chest cavity as if a small stereo had been placed exactly where your heart should be. The constant noise and pressure was sometimes pierced by a scream or a shriek as fans cheered or battled with one another. When my usher turned to leave, I nearly reached out and grabbed his arm, wanting someone, *anyone*, to stay here with me. No one else from my dad's gym was here, so the two seats next to me, draped with a reserved ribbon, sat empty. I crossed and uncrossed my legs, looking up at the boxing ring. The blue leather shone out from under the lights and the bright red ropes looked like giant licorice strips, bounding one space so uniquely from the rest of the arena.

"Ladies and gentlemen..." A low, sultry voice bellowed from what felt like the concrete floor itself and sent a hush over the crowd. It was wild, seeing this frenetic place transform as the anticipation of the main event flooded throughout. My heart started pounding so hard, I could hear the rush of blood in my ears. I wanted to text Toni and tell her how utterly insane this was but I couldn't seem to move my hands. I felt frozen in place.

"Tonight is a very special evening indeed. We have two new fighters. Two highly anticipated and evenly matched fighters. Blood will be shed, my good friends. The question is, who will black out first?" The crowd went absolutely wild at the announcer's words while the color drained completely from my face. How did Toni like this shit? I could barely get an ugly bruise or stand the sight of blood in a hospital setting. How was I going to sit just feet away from a ring in which blood and blackouts were basically guaranteed? Booking flights and cars, ensuring travel details were arranged for and schedules kept across time zones all felt so benign. So, professional. But this? This felt like the modern-day Colosseum. Like these people wanted to see blood and lions and gladiators and they weren't' planning on leaving with anything less. I felt my stomach roil but as the lights darkened, I also felt excitement. No one knew me here. Better yet, no one even knew I was here. Tonight would be something I'd never forget, and no one had to know.

"Please, without further ado..." the commentator dragged on his announcement even as his words conveyed the opposite, "let's welcome the lithe, athletic, never-tiring...Nico Chavez!" His words blurred with the screams and shouts of the crowd. A single spotlight cut through the darkness, growing in intensity as it traveled toward the ring. Nico's long, athletic body was outlined in light, his dark head bowed and his skin slick with oil. He looked larger than life, even hotter than seeing him up close. He finally pulled his head up, as if he'd finished some sort of prayer or meditation, and gazed out at the audience, a single line of energy seeming to emanate from his body directly into the crowd. Everyone could feel it. His power, his eagerness to be in the ring. Then his head turned in my direction. His eyes connected with mine. I didn't move an inch. At first, Nico remained an elegant statue, giving no indication that he acknowledged my presence. But then he winked. At me. And a dimple appeared in the smooth olive skin of his cheek.

## NICO

Jabs, combinations, punch sequences, breathing techniques. These are all the things I know. The things I've been trained to know, not only in my mind but in my body. Learned instinct. But this? Standing under the heat of the spotlights with people screaming my name from every corner of a black and vast arena was entirely foreign. I didn't know what to do with my arms, my face. Where to look, how to act. And then I saw her. The only person in the front-row on my side. And I'd wink. I had actually full-on *winked* at her like a goddamn douchebag. I don't think I'd ever winked at a girl in my life.

But she was here, looking unsure and porcelain as hell, hardly moving an inch in her seat when the rest of the arena was writhing with energy. I was grateful when the heat of the spotlight and the respective crowd's attention was shifted from me to my opponent, using the moment to center myself in the darkness of my ring corner. I knew this was a taste of what Rhett had been alluding to; the side of this business that couldn't be taught in hours of sparring but could only be learned by doing. The showmanship, the ability to control my emotions and my nerves. A part of me, a large part, knew I was ready. But the other part of me had no fucking idea what I was doing. My only choice was to fight like hell to find my way through it.

"And now, it is time..." the announcer dragged on every word, my muscles coiling tighter, "for round one!" The sound of the bell slammed into his final word as if the two were one and before I saw it coming, my opponent was rushing me like a rabid dog. He wasted no time crowding my personal space, his strong and burly figure wrapping itself around my waist in a wrestler's move. My limbs froze and my mind went black as I heard the embarrassing sound of my back hitting the mat like I was staring down at my own body. *Christ, I'd already lost round one.* My opponent pushed himself off of me with a grunt, and I quickly leapt up from the floor, trying to block out the boos and discordant sounds from the crowd. I did a quick rib check. Everything was fine. Everything but my fucking ego. I bounced a few times on my calves, staring straight into empty space as I cleared my thoughts and envisioned only the energy from my muscles running through me.

This time when the bell rang out, I stayed on my toes. My opponent went for the same tactic and I quickly evaded his thick arms, getting a few punches into his kidneys from behind. He didn't back away or give himself space, but instead moved closer into my punches, still trying to get at my waist. We were tightly locked, our movements hard to decipher for the crowd, but each of my punches landed solidly in his ribs or kidneys while he tried in vain to wrap himself around me again. But my arms were too fast and moving too rhythmically. I left no openings for him to take advantage. I finally landed a punch so hard and fluid, I could hear the loss of air from my opponent's chest as he grabbed his own waist with his arms, trying to keep himself upright. Within seconds he fell to his knees, one hand gripping his side while the other was palm down on the mat, holding himself upright. I looked out at the crowd, almost checking to see if they were still there like a little kid in a bad dream. I wasn't used to this scale of arena. Or really any arena for that matter. Even the biggest underground ones lacked the scale and polish of this place. I ambled back to my corner, not sure what else to do, and gulped down a few precious sips of water before the bell sounded again for round 3.

The rest of the fight was equally matched back and forth. I won two rounds in a row, and then my opponent had a comeback and brought me down on the mat hard, the side of my head smashing aggressively into the floor, pain throbbing in both temples. Sparring never hurt this fucking bad. When I stood up, my vision was slightly blurry but I wasn't tired. That was always the main thing I had going for me. When my opponents started to get weary, their muscles tensing and their breathing becoming more labored, I seemed to go into overdrive. Fighting was the only way I could coral that energy for good and suppress the anxiety and the mania that lived within me. It felt right, it *was* right that I spent my energy this way. That was the only way I could explain it.

When the bell rang out, I circled my opponent, showing off my limitless energy compared to his more wary and tiring figure. I could tell that just watching me exhausted him. He tried to barrel after me a few times, but I was too quick. The activity soon became frustrating to the crowd who wanted to see blood, not defensive maneuvers. When he barreled toward me another time, instead of twisting out his reach, I caught his fist by surprise and twisted it back while using my other hand to get an uppercut straight to his jaw. The length of my arms kept him far enough away from my core that I had the full advantage. I punched longer than I needed to, my forceful contact with his body keeping him upright, but it felt good. I needed to exhaust myself, to leave it all on the mat of my first fight. Especially after my embarrassingly quick defeat in round one. Finally his heavy knees hit the mat, followed by his torso, his bear-like body slumping into a sweat mound at my feet. The cheers were deafening and I looked out in wonder at the crowd whose faces I couldn't see. I felt myself smiling, an unsure but genuine grin spreading over my face as the voice in my head repeated itself over and over, "Nico, you won. You won."

## 23

## MEREDITH

I didn't have enough time to fully grasp what had just happened. My hands were shaking with adrenaline when the usher who had initially seated me was back at my side, gripping my upper arm lightly.

"We have a booth reserved at Copper Club. 2nd floor, VIP. What time should we expect Nico?" His body was lean, his vibe the artist type, but his hold on my arm was strong. We were moving quickly past the ring, the smell of sweat invading my nostrils and the sounds of the overly excited arena rushing past my ears as I tried to focus.

"I'm sorry, what? I--I don't understand."

"The after party. For Nico. We need to know how many others the bodyguards should let in. I'd guess 20?"

My head was spinning. I hadn't realized that party planning was another part of my duties as tour manager. And I hadn't even been to a party since *that* night. The night when Hewitt got me so high and then framed me for a tragedy that I knew wasn't my fault but was also starting to believe that I wasn't completely innocent either. It was like an anchor around my neck, dragging me under the salty water's surface every time my mind went there.

"You are Meredith, right? Nico's tour manager?" The usher threw open a heavy steel door, moving us into a much quieter hallway.

"Uh, yes. Yes, I am. Sorry. I'm just--" before I could finish my sentence Nico's body emerged at the other end of the hall. His olive skin was slick with sweat, his hair pushed back off his forehead like he'd just run his fingers through it. And then I spotted them. Two beautiful women, one on each side, hanging onto his arms. Nico was smiling but there was a tightness to his facial expression. I didn't know him well enough to read his emotions.

"Nico! Well done, my man. I'm Chase. I help run this arena. You've got a wild night ahead of you." The usher, apparently named Chase, offered Nico his fist for a bump. "You ladies coming too?" They both giggled and flipped their hair, one of them looking me up and down with an unmistakable catty expression on her face.

"Is this your girlfriend?" The girl gestured lazily toward me, not taking her arm off of Nico's, and I slitted my greens at her rude tone.

"What? Woah, no. No, she's Coach's daughter." Nico stuttered out a raspy explanation, laughing nervously before he swallowed hard, his strong neck bobbing with the movement.

"Coach's who?" Chase looked between us, confused. "I thought you said you were his tour manager?"

"I am." I tried to ignore how quick Nico was to disregard that there'd be any chance I was his girlfriend. I flipped my dark red hair over my shoulder, falling into my ice bitch mode. It was my defense mechanism in all uncomfortable situations. And this definitely qualified as one of those. "My dad is the head coach at Nico's gym. And I'm Nico's tour manager. Is that too complicated to understand?"

"Jeez, relax." The other girl rolled her eyes at me, leaning further into Nico's side. Nico's eyes widened in response, the look of discomfort on his face growing by the second.

"They're not on the Copper Club invite list." I looked directly at Chase, as I pointed at the girls, not missing how childish I was being, but still not able to stop myself. Sometimes you had to get your wins where you could.

"Um, what!" The girls dropped their hold on Nico's arm, a petulant look on their pretty, made up faces.

"Whatever you say, boss." Chase looked at me, holding up his hands in mock surrender, something like admiration crossing over his face. I gave him a tight smile before turning back to Nico.

"You need to shower."

"Yes." Nico still looked like a deer in the headlights. A tall, sexy, rippling with muscle deer in the headlights.

"We will head out in twenty. Where can I wait until we're ready to go to the club?" I turned back to Chase in my full boss mode.

"I'll take you to the lounge. Nico, your prep room is on the way." The three of us started moving further down the hallway.

"Um, what about us?" We stopped briefly and turned back to face the two women, their lips pouty and their arms crossed over their chests.

"The party's at Copper Club. You can wait in line." I gave them a little smirk before turning back around. My phone started buzzing in my pocket but I let it go to voicemail.

## 24

# NICO

The hot water felt good on my back, slicing through the tension of my muscles after tonight's fight. I was excited that I'd won and the slew of congratulatory texts from the gym had my phone vibrating non-stop. I knew that Rhett and Coach Barry felt bad at not being able to attend my first fight, but part of me was glad they'd missed it. That first round was embarrassing as hell. I should've had my opponent up against the ropes in a second, rather than the other way around. And even though I could rest easier tonight knowing I'd landed my first W on tour, it shouldn't have been as hard as it was. But Rhett had been right: there was only so much you could train for in the gym. The screaming fans, the hot spotlights of the arena, the showmanship? That was just something you had to experience firsthand in order to learn. And even Rhett hadn't been as exposed to this level of theatre in the underground. This was the big-time. Fully legit, sanctioned. Big posters and campaigns advertising the event to fighting junkies and transient entertainment seekers alike. I had never thought of myself as an *entertainer.* I mean, this wasn't fake WWE stuff, but there was still an element of stardom that you had to bring into the ring. I felt like a goddamn fish out of water. I closed my eyes and let the run rush over me, washing the embarrassment and frustration of that first round out of my mind. But I knew what kept the loop going in my head. It was the fact that Meredith had seen it all, front freaking row. I was the one who'd asked her to come so I only had myself to blame.

I turned off the shower and towel dried my hair and my chest, pulling on the plain white t-shirt and jeans that I'd packed for after the fight. I knew my lessons of being a fighter on tour weren't over yet. Tonight would be my first after-party. The exact environment Coach Barry had warned me about. It was the reason Rhett didn't last in these kinds of tournaments. Not because of his lack of skill, the guy was a monster in the ring. But because he hadn't been able to keep his nose clean with all the temptations. These after parties were like throwing forbidden meat into a hungry lion's cage. Sure, you could get away with it, and plenty of fighters did, but there were always people laying traps for you to get caught. Opponents trying to sabotage you with drugs and women. Trying to get you thrown out before you even stepped foot into the ring. I'd promised Coach Barry I could handle it. Now I just needed to uphold that promise to myself. I'd never been interested in any of this crazy party stuff anyway, but I'd also never been exposed to it. I looked at my reflection in the mirror, flashes of my sisters coming to my mind. That's why I was here. For them. For us. I'd have fun and learn this way of life. But I wouldn't let myself lose focus. I wouldn't be another fighter in a long list of talent who had thrown it all away for a good time. I wouldn't be that guy. *Right?*

"Nico! Car's waiting!" I heard Chase yell through the

door of my prepping room and put my hotel key and phone in my jeans pocket. I let out a slow breath through my nose, forcing myself to play it cool.

"Coming." I opened the door and nodded at Chase, glancing around and noticing that Meredith wasn't with him.

"Where's Meredith?"

"She's already on her way to the club. She'll help manage the crowd." I nodded, not really knowing what that meant and wondering if Meredith really did either. Both of us were totally new to this world but she handled herself like a pro earlier, as if she'd been doing this shit for years.

"Hey by the way," Chase and I started walking down the hallway, his eyes focused on his phone as he quickly typed out a text, "your tour manager, Meredith...is she single? I've always had a thing for redheads."

I cleared my throat before responding. "Uh, I actually don't know." That was the truth. I didn't know. But I regretted my response as soon as the words were out of my mouth. This guy would only be around for one night since he managed this arena. I could've told him Meredith was freaking married and he'd never know.

"Hey, better than nothing." He winked at me and I felt an uncomfortable pit settle in my stomach. *Was this guy Meredith's type?* We didn't say anything else as we made our way outside and into the black car waiting for us. No doubt, another well-timed arrangement made by Meredith.

"My guy at the club texted me. Looks like you'll have a lot of tens to choose from."

"What?" I slid into the backseat, my head swimming with confusion as screaming fans moved chaotically around the car, a few iPhone cameras flashing.

"Tens. Dimes. Hot as hell women waiting to jump your

bones," Chase cocked his head at me like I was his younger brother. The thought was ironic considering I had at least eighty pounds on him, not to mention my professionally trained fists. "Don't worry, bro, you'll get used to it." The car pulled out into the road, loud rap music blaring over the speakers.

## 25

## MEREDITH

The Copper Club was so loud it was hard to hear my own thoughts. I was sitting in the VIP lounge, sectioned off by thick, dark red velvet ropes with a balcony-style view overlooking the dance floor. I'd been to a few clubs during college, the ones that would accept fake IDs anyway, but this was another level. I felt like I was in a movie. But of course, I didn't let that sense of awe show on my face. I glanced down at my phone and saw the slew of texts from Toni who was demanding play by play updates but I'd have to deal with that later. God, I wished she was here right now. She'd remind me of how fun and badass this was instead of me feeling like a freaking out-of-place wall-flower. Just like back in highschool. My default was to go into work mode. I checked my ever-growing to-do list and triple-checked the flight arrangements for our next stop after Philadelphia. This travel schedule was brutal. It was going to be exhausting for me, let alone for Nico who had to actually fight almost every other night. I'd heard from Ava that some of the big-time fighters that had been doing this for years had private planes and chefs and physical therapists. Nico just had me. And that was turning out to be a hell of a lot of pressure.

My phone started vibrating again but I was distracted by the parade of long legs and beautiful hair as one of the bouncers opened the ropes to let eight or nine women inside the VIP space, their faces picture-perfect and excited. For one moment I wished I could just be one of them. To only know Nico from a distance as the hot fighter that he was and not the young man whose burgeoning career was somehow my responsibility for the next several months. Maybe this whole thing was a bad idea. My attempt at avoiding one painful situation may have landed me smackdab in another one. The women sat on the couches, touching up their makeup and placing drink orders with our designated hostess.

"What would you like to drink?" The hostess made her way over to me, her smile friendly.

"I'll have sparkling water. With lime." I glanced back down at my phone, pretending to check my work list.

"You're not drinking? That's a first." Her tone was kind but she didn't leave.

"I'm the tour manager." I cocked my head slightly, needing to convey for the second time tonight that I wasn't just trying to sleep with a fighter but that this was my actual job.

"Ahh, gotcha. Most of the tour managers don't look like you." She winked before heading away. I noticed all of the women looking in a certain direction and moved my gaze in the direction of theirs.

Nico was following Chase, towering nearly two feet above him. He was wearing a perfectly fitted white t-shirt, outlining every nuance of his strong, lean body. I'd never seen him in jeans and now I really, really wished that I hadn't. He looked painfully handsome. I felt my breath catch in my throat. The women started to move closer toward him and I was brought back to reality. My phone started to pulse again in my hand and this time I was grateful for the distraction. I stood up to find a quieter place, my eyes locking with Nico for only a moment as I raised the phone to my ear and ducked my head, signaling to the bouncer that I needed to take a call. He led me down a quiet hallway off to the side, closing the door behind him.

"Hello?" I twirled my hair distractedly, still seeing the image of Nico surrounded by those women.

"About time you stop ignoring me," the blood drained from my face as Hewitt's voice came over the phone. My throat felt like it was clogged with sand. I couldn't respond.

"Don't hang up," his voice was anxious, which ratched my own anxiety even higher, "I know I put you in a shit position. I shouldn't have done that. But I miss you. And," he paused before continuing, "I need one more favor. I have a delivery due and the cops are onto me. Watching me like a hawk. Someone snitched. Probably that fucker Truman. I have to lay low. But these guys, my supplier, they don't fuck around. They--"

"No." I couldn't keep the word from forcefully rushing from my mouth. I'd heard this all before. And it landed me here. Outside of a VIP lounge in Philadelphia where I'd fled after getting suspended from college. A suspension that was due to Hewitt and his lies. I wasn't going to take the fall for him again.

"Listen, Meredith. You don't get to just say 'no.' You were there. You saw him die and you didn't do anything. You're just as guilty as me." My veins froze at his words, a slight shiver taking over me. Flashes of that night came back to me painfully and I tried to suppress the nausea in my stomach.

"No, I'm not. I was high, Hewitt, you got all of us high and--"

"And you didn't want to get in trouble. You didn't want to call the cops because then you'd be arrested for drugs too. And you let Asher die--"

"You let him die!" My voice was a scream and I couldn't contain my emotion any longer. "I told you before I took whatever you gave me that we should get Asher help. And then...I got so high, I couldn't even form words, let alone call for help."

"Your word against mine, Meredith. Your word against mine, and you're the one who got caught trying to sell drugs on campus. Who do you think the cops will believe, Meredith? A suspended bitchy privileged girl or the captain of the varsity basketball team?" His words hit me in the gut, and I felt like Nico's opponents, getting slain right where it hurt the most. I hung up the phone, my hand trembling. I heard a knock on the door and I jumped, grasping my chest with my hand before opening the door slowly, part of me afraid that Hewitt would be standing right outside that door. That he'd already found me.

"Meredith, you okay?" Nico's handsome face was etched with concern, his bicep protruding through the thin fabric of his white t-shirt as he braced himself against the doorway.

"I'm, I'm fine. Excuse me." *How much of that conversation had Nico heard?* I brushed past him and nodded to the bouncer. It was time for more than sparkling water. A lot more.

## 26

### MEREDITH

I waved down our hostess and ordered a vodka soda with the added request to keep them coming. Nico and I didn't fly out of Philadelphia until after 1:00 PM tomorrow, and with how violently my hands were shaking, I knew I wouldn't be able to resist the welcome buzz of alcohol to numb my reaction after my call with Hewitt.

"Meredith," Nico was right behind me as I took a huge gulp of my first drink.

"Nico," I forced myself to swallow, "you won! You won your first fight, you should celebrate. This," I gestured around the dimly lit VIP area, all of the female guests eyeing Nico longingly as he towered over me, "is your celebration. So, celebrate." My smile felt as fake as it looked but the more alcohol I got into my system the more genuine it would become. Nico had only seen annoyed Meredith. Nervous, type-A, bitchy ice-princess Meredith. But he hadn't seen party Meredith. The fun-loving girl deep inside of me who got herself into trouble just as soon as she emerged. Hewitt knew it. He sought me out specifically for it. I would never let someone take advantage of me like that again. But that didn't mean I couldn't do it to myself.

"You sure you're okay?" Nico moved in impossibly closer and I felt myself audibly gulp as I took another healthy drink of my vodka soda. He smelled like pine. Freshly showered and masculine.

"Yes, Nico. I'm fine. Tonight's just been...a lot. I mean, that was my first fight ever and this is my first real club and-
-"

"Yeah, tell me about it." Nico sighed deeply before plopping down on the velvet sofa behind me, seemingly oblivious to all of the female stares in his direction as they stirred their cocktails and whispered anxiously in each other's ears about Nico.

"What do you mean?" I sat down next to him, mindful to keep a big enough difference between us as to appear professional without making it painfully obvious that being too close to him made me and my hormones nervous as hell. *You work for him, Meredith. Keep it together.*

"I'm just saying, those firsts are my firsts too. I mean, I've sparred more times than I can count. But tonight," he shook his head, one thick dark wave of hair falling free from his combed back style and laying across his tanned forehead, "that was something else. And this...this whole club scene...yeah, I'd rather be back at the hotel. Eating a pizza or something. This shit makes me nervous. Why are they all...just staring at me like that?"

I laughed at his comment like he'd just told me an embarrassing secret and that same dimple appeared in his cheek that I'd seen from the front row when he smiled and winked at me before the fight. Nico was charming, but in a way that made you realize he didn't fully understand just how charming he was. He wasn't oblivious, but he was so in his own head, trying to work hard and not fuck up that you knew his charm wasn't an act. The thought made my stomach flip thinking about the den of women wanting to hook up with him, mere feet away from us, just for the stigma of being with a hot, up and coming fighter. Sex for the bragging rights. Or maybe to even hitch a free ride on tour. The thought made me shift uncomfortably in my seat.

"Look, I wasn't trying to insult you or any of the planning you've done. You've been a total pro, it's really impressive actually. I'm sure I'll get better at this club scene."

I laughed softly and set my nearly empty drink down on the coffee table. "Hey, I can't take the credit for the club, only for arranging the car to get you here. This was all," I paused for a moment blanking on the artsy usher's name from the arena.

"Chase." Nico filled in the blank but he was no longer looking at me. I turned in the direction of his stare and saw Chase chatting with the bouncer, making his way easily past the red ropes. Chase was *that* guy. The one who knew everyone and everything in a certain place. He'd been brusque but somehow comforting when I'd felt like a total fish out of water in the arena and I was happy to see another guest in the room that wasn't an insanely gorgeous model-looking VIP pick for Nico. You know, just for variety's sake.

"Ah, there's my lovely redhead." Chase came over to us, his movements jaunty as he leaned over and kissed my cheek. The whole thing felt very grown-up, like I was *someone* in a city with the people who *knew people* and not just the suspended former wallflower who got caught up with the wrong guy in college. Chase flopped down beside me, draping his arm lazily over the back of the sofa and throwing up his pointer finger at the hostess to get her attention.

"Gin and tonic. With lime. Also, tell the pirate that the bird has landed." Chase quickly dismissed the hostess and turned back to me, a confused expression on my face.

"Who's the pirate?" I scrunch my nose in confusion, polishing off the last of my drink.

"The one with all the treasure." Chase winked at me but it fell flat compared to Nico's. Before I could ask anything else, I felt Nico's large, warm hand over mine, a startling bolt of electricity flooding through my arm and into my chest.

"Let's get out of here." His voice was low and his expression looked wary.

"Nico, we just got here. Really, it's fine, we don't have to--"

"I promised," his jaw started to tick, a tension taking over his face that I hadn't seen before, "I promised Rhett and Coach that I wouldn't--" He looked at Chase and then back at me, lowering his voice even further, "I promised your *dad* that I wouldn't do any drugs. And there's no way in hell I'm having you around that shit either."

"Who said anything about drugs?" My voice was a high-pitched whisper and my heart started to race. Images flooded back of that night, seeing Asher's body slumping further into the sofa, the skin of his face turning glassy and impossibly blue. *I should've called for help...*

"The pirate is a dealer and treasure is coke...or something even worse. I'm not positive but I'm pretty damn sure. Grew up around enough druggies to spot one." Nico gripped my hand tighter and pulled me into his side as he stood up.

"Woah, wait up!" Chase leapt up from the sofa, his drink nearly sloshing out of his hand, "Where the hell are you two going, the party hasn't even started yet. Nico, take your pick buddy. Doesn't even have to be just one." Chase wiggled his eyebrows suggestively and I wanted to slap him across the face. Nico leaned in closer to him, his neck nearly brushing against my cheek as the scent of pine overwhelmed me.

"All yours, buddy." Nico tapped Chase's chest good-naturedly but his entire expression and tone was nothing short of threatening. Before I could say anything else, Nico was pulling me past the velvet ropes and down the stairs, a flutter of nerves and excitement that I knew shouldn't be there, blooming in my chest.

## 27

# NICO

I resisted the urge to reach out and touch Meredith's mesmerizing thick red hair as she started making her way down the stairs from VIP when I felt a hand on my back.

"Hey, bro, what the hell?" Chase was behind me, a grin trying to mask the true look of annoyance on his face. "I arranged this whole thing for you and I...well I was planning on making a move on pretty little Ariel over there." He grinned wolfishly, the look showing how thin and strained his face was, covered in a patchy beard.

"She's Coach's daughter," My words were a growl and Meredith turned around to face me, her eyes confused as she realized I was still near the top of the stairs.

"Coach's daughter my ass, I don't know the coach." Chase laughed and I realized that the, *"she's Coach's daughter"* loop that had been on repeat in my head every time I looked at Meredith too long or thought about her too much was a warning better kept to myself than said out loud.

"Look man, we're leaving. Gotta fly out early tomorrow." I gritted my teeth in a combination of anger and embarrassment as Meredith held up her hands as if to ask what was taking so long. I didn't wait for Chase to reply before I jogged down the steps with my hands in my pockets, keeping my head down.

"Should we call an Uber?" Meredith glanced up at me on the sidewalk, the wind blowing her hair wildly around her face.

"You usually arrange the rides," I winked at her and wished that I had a jacket to offer her against the wind. She smiled back at me, a light blush creeping over her cheeks as she pulled out her phone. By the time we got back to the hotel I was starving, my stomach growling loudly.

"Hungry boy?" Meredith glanced at me over her shoulder, setting her purse down on the small bar that joined the kitchenette with the rest of the suite.

"No one ever accused me of not being able to eat." I plopped down on the sofa, my muscles feeling sore from the jerky and reactionary moves you make in the ring that you don't make nearly as often when sparring. I started to massage my shoulder blades, the pain settling in.

"You sore?" Meredith sat down at the edge of the sofa, a look of professional concern on her face.

"Yeah, can you give me a massage?" I wiggled my eyebrows at her jokingly, not at all expecting her to actually do it. I mean, some of the really famous guys on tour that had been doing this for years had personal massage therapists and teams but I'd have to work my way up to that. Besides, having that big of a team and that many people around me kind of freaked me out. I wasn't used to all the attention. Including the attention from tonight.

"Um," Meredith cleared her throat and stood up from the couch, "I mean, I guess. You know, if you're in pain then sure I can try. Not sure I'm any good..."

"Joking. Just a joke," I sat up straighter, bracing my elbows on my knees, "need to work on my sense of humor."

"Or maybe I need to work on mine." Meredith laughed lightly like she was finally releasing a tension that had been inside of her all night.

"I'm still hungry though." I made my face serious and she giggled. God, what a sweet sound. *Coach's. Daughter.*

"Well, let's get room service. You won tonight, you earned it. The contract covers things like this," Meredith gave me a mischievous look as she thumbed through the leatherbound room service menu.

"Do they have pizza?"

"Hmm, looks more like a scallops and steak kind of menu."

"Poor taste." Meredith giggled at my response and set the room service menu down, reaching for her phone.

"You better not be a pineapple and ham on pizza kind of guy."

"Woah," I held up my hands in mock surrender, "no need to go straight for the jugular. Do I really give off Hawaian pizza vibes? Pepperoni only. Classic. I'm a simple man, Meredith." This time her giggle turned into a full-on laugh and watching the ice-princess I'd come to know thaw around the edges made it that much harder to *not* feel anything. To not want to run my fingers through her hair and pull the back of her head towards me. To feel the vibration of her laugh against my lips...

"Large pepperoni and cheese pizza. Coming right up, boss." She smiled brightly at me before turning back to her phone but the word, *boss,* caught me off guard. This girl wasn't here *with* me, she's here *for* me. For a job. For a job that I still didn't fully understand why she took. Before I could overthink any further, I felt my phone vibrate in my pocket.

"Celeste?" I stood up slowly, immediately thinking something must be wrong if my sister was calling me this late. Meredith gave me a strange look that I couldn't decipher. "What's wrong? You okay?"

"Yes, Nico, relax. I'm fine. We're fine. I just wanted to congratulate you! Ava texted me and let me know that you won tonight. That's amazing. I wish I could've seen it." The tension in my body slowly dissipated at hearing that everything back home was fine but I cringed inwardly at the thought of my younger sister anywhere near tonight's fight. Even though Celeste couldn't have been more than a few years younger than Meredith, she seemed way more innocent or delicate to me since I'd known her since she was a baby. It had been my responsibility to protect her, and Maria too, for so many years. I'd never want her seeing me violent and crazed in the ring like I was tonight.

"Thanks, yeah, it was good to win the first one," I glanced over at Meredith who looked like she was trying to ignore me but I couldn't tell, "how's Maria? Not giving you any trouble?" I heard a scuffle over the phone and then Maria's sweet voice came on the line.

"Nico! I'm being the bestest I've ever been, ever. You made me pinky promise!" I smiled at hearing her squeal and felt a slight ache at not being able to throw her over my shoulder and tickle her until she kicked like a maniac. I loved that little monster, especially since she was still a few years out from the teenage years. Those were the worst.

"Stay safe, okay?" Celeste came back on the phone, taking on the adult role.

"I will. Talk soon." I hung up and looked over at Meredith who appeared to be absorbed in her phone.

"Sisters." I shrugged before falling back on the couch, trying to play casual but also knowing there was a reason I made a point to mention exactly who I was and wasn't talking to. And it wasn't a good reason. *Coach. Barry's. Only. Daughter.*

"You have sisters?" Her eyes locked on mine, a look of unmistakable relief on her face.

"Two. Feels like ten." Meredith's giggle made a reappearance and I knew for a fact that she had been jealous. At least a little bit. I tried to suppress my satisfaction, knowing giving into it would only mean trouble.

"Pizza should be here in ten."

"You get a large?"

"Yep." She sat down on the couch again, not close enough to touch me but not as far away as before at the club.

"Good. So, what are you going to eat?" Meredith's jaw popped open and I couldn't help but laugh at her expression.

"You're not going to eat a large pizza all by yourself, Nico."

"Is that a dare?" Meredith shook her head, a sweet smile spreading across her porcelain face, the ice princess facade melting just a bit further.

## 28

## MEREDITH

My cheeks were warm. *Too warm.* I went into the bathroom to get a little space from the electricity and heat that was Nico. I felt like my body was buzzing and needed to take a few deep breaths to calm down. How could a girl not be affected by a man like him? He was sweet and funny and didn't try to control the room. Except when he was in the ring. Then he was in total control, finding his sense of power with each round, his long strong limbs striking out like an animal coming into their full instinctual potential. The contrast between his two modes was disarming. And it was affecting me. *Pizza. Pizza was what friends did, right? We'd eat and then go to bed. Me on the couch of course.*

When the pizza arrived I reconsidered whether Nico saying he could eat the whole thing by himself had ever really been a joke at all. He downed nearly a half of it before even looking up at me.

"Sorry. You want a piece?" He wiped the corner of his mouth, his tongue darting out over his bottom lip in a flash. He held the piece out to me like he was offering something far more than food. But that was just my mind going to places it had no business going.

"Sure," I took the pizza from him, my stomach suddenly very much *not* hungry. It felt twisted up in knots, the heat coming back into my cheeks as I folded my legs underneath me and sat cross-legged on the couch, taking baby bites of the slice. I could only get halfway through before setting it down. "Maybe I should learn to cook, before you get an actual cook on your team? Or set up a meal service for you? Ava mentioned some of the fighters do that." Nico leaned his head back, resting it against the sofa. He was so long and tall, taking up all the space in the room in a way that I loved but also made me incredibly nervous at the same time. Why did he feel so close even though he was an entire arm's length away?

He closed his eyes, "Pizza is good. You don't need to do anything else, you've been great." I catch a sigh before it escapes my lips, taking advantage of his closed eyes to scan down his long body, his t-shirt and jeans only accentuating the delicious and toned muscles that I knew were beneath. He turned towards me quickly, his eyes opening in time to catch me blatantly checking him out. The smirk that crawled slowly across his face felt like it was touching me, burning me, everywhere.

"I have?" My words were a whisper. I didn't know where the rest of my voice had gone. I didn't actually need his validation about my work. I knew I was doing fine and I also knew that in a mere few months he'd have a fully professional tour manager onboard, giving him exactly what he needed. I was temporary, transitory, but I still wanted to hear him compliment again. Even if I was giving it way too much weight.

"Hell, yeah. You're..." He sat up straighter, running a hand through his messy hair, "impressive."

"Ha, I'm not the one who got a fancy fighting tour contract. You're impressive." He cast his eyes down, before looking back up at me. He didn't look flattered or confident. Instead, he looked worried. Doubtful.

"I hope so. I mean, I have to be. I don't have a choice. My sisters, Rhett, Coach...they're all counting on me. It's a lot of pressure." His mention of Coach brought me back a little closer to reality that he was talking about *my dad* after all. But I barely even knew my dad. I didn't *feel* like the coach's daughter even if that's how Nico would always think of me.

"They believe in you. I mean, who wouldn't?"

"Do you?" His dark eyes practically glittered. The tension on his handsome face made me feel like my answer was important to him. More important than anyone else's.

"Yes." I was surprised he could even hear me, my voice was so faint. Nico slid a few inches closer to me, slowly. Almost as if he was expecting me to get up from the couch. I didn't move. We locked eyes and could only hear the sounds of our breathing, not saying another word.

Nico moved closer again, this time with more confidence. I felt like a deer in the headlights. Even if I wanted to move, I wouldn't have been able to. The electricity emanating from him was so strong, I physically felt pulled to it. The force too powerful to resist. He rested his strong arm across the back of the couch behind my head. His forearm was inches from my cheek but he still wasn't touching me.

"I know you must hear this all the goddamn time," his neck moved in an insanely masculine way as he swallowed hard, the combination of his manliness and boyish nerves throwing my hormones into overdrive, "but you are so beautiful. It makes me nervous as hell." I felt all the air leave my chest and my mouth went completely dry. I would kill for a glass of water right now but there was no way I was leaving this couch. I wanted to speak but my throat wasn't working so I just stared back at him, my eyes not leaving his.

"Meredith," his voice was part pleading, part hypnotizing. He was so close I could feel his warm breath on my skin, his lips just a fraction away from mine. "I really want to kiss you right now." The way he said the words were like he'd already given up. Like he was expecting me to say no. I didn't say anything. I wanted him to kiss me too. *Needed* him to do it. When I still didn't speak or move, he smiled briefly, casting his eyes down and that damn dimple appearing in his check. "Say something, anything, if you want me to stop."

I stared back at him, my eyes unwavering from his. I didn't even want to sigh or swallow or blink for fear that he'd interrupt that as some sort of verbal response. Some indicator that I wanted him to stop. He waited one more long moment before closing the distance between us, his lips touching mine gently at first and then with more pressure. The arm on the back of the couch moved slowly into my hair, curling around the back of my neck as he pressed me deeper into him, into the kiss. I felt his tongue move into my mouth and the deep, satisfied groan from the back of his throat had me moving closer to him, wrapping my hands around his neck. My hands were shaking but I was too enamoured to be embarrassed.

Nico's other hand slid around my hip, pulling me slowly down the couch and putting the weight of his body over mine. He braced himself once I was laying flat, one palm getting the full weight of his muscles hovering above me, never breaking our kiss. I felt like I was drowning. It wasn't in a panicky way, but in total acceptance. If this was how I was going out, then so be it. I'd succumb. It was nice to not be putting up a wall. To just let go and let someone in. Quite literally Nico in my mouth, in my hair, in my space. He slid his hand down over my thigh, caressing gently before his grip became more firm and he wrapped my leg around his hip, my calf resting on his lower back. It was like he was wrapping me around him, the heat almost too painful to endure.

"Tell me to stop, Meredith." His lips touched mine as he spoke, his face too close for me to see his eyes. I said nothing. My chest rose heavily as I greedily sucked in whatever air I could before his lips were on mine again. He moved his hand over the waistband of my jeans, his fingers grazing over my zipper. I felt my body freeze. A sense of coolness and alarm replacing the electricity of his touch. I closed my eyes knowing the thought that was creeping into my head. Knowing the thought before it fully formed and hating it with every fiber of my being. I thought of *him.* Of Hewitt. The last boy who had touched me. The only person who had hurt me so deeply the scars would never heal. Not because I'd loved him, but because I'd trusted him. With my body, with my life. And he'd used it all against me. Nico stopped kissing me, planting his palms firmly beside my head and lifting himself off of me. My leg fell limply from his hip. I wanted to scream. I wanted to cry. I thought I already hated Hewitt before, but now it was an entirely new level of hate. It was resentment. I didn't want the thought of Hewitt anywhere near Nico and his hands and his dimple and the way he made me feel like a giddy teenager. I pushed the thoughts down, reaching back for Nico, wanting to bring him back to me. Needing his touch to push away the thought of Hewitt. But Nico was already gone. His dark eyes were laced with regret and I would have done anything to replace that look with the lust he'd had for me earlier.

"Fuck." Nico bit out the word like it was bitter on his tongue. I'd never heard him sound like that before. "I'm so sorry, Meredith. I knew I shouldn't have. I mean, Jesus, your dad trusted me and..." He didn't finish his thought as he lifted himself off of me and stood up from the couch. "You're Coach's daughter and I crossed a line. I'm sorry." He looked defeated like he'd lost a fight in the ring. I sat up on my elbows knowing I'd already ruined this, whatever *this* was. Nico clearly thought my apprehension was because of my dad. Better left that way than to know the truth. He went into the bathroom and closed the door behind him, my heart racing with anxiety and anger. I stood up and brushed my hair down, cleaning up our pizza and plates to do something with my hands which were still shaking. I started making up a bed on the couch, not wanting Nico to think there was any way he wasn't sleeping in the bed. He was the one who needed the rest. Besides, at this rate, I'd be up all night.

## 29

# NICO

We barely spoke a word to one another during the entire flight. Meredith had her ice princess shield back up in full force and I didn't feel like it was my right to even try and thaw it out. I'd crossed a line. A huge, red, glaring line that had been perfectly in place all along. This was a distraction. *She* was a distraction. And distractions weren't something that I could afford during this tour.

When we landed, a black car was waiting for us and we slid into the backseat, careful not to touch each other. I wish it had just been a momentary thing, a lapse in judgement. But the attraction between us was thick in the air. At least the air I was breathing. It was impossible to tell with Meredith. Her icy blue-green eyes fixed on the back of the driver's headrest like it was the most interesting thing in the world. I opened my mouth to try and break the awkward silence when Meredith's phone started to ring.

"Hey, dad." Her voice was professional, not giving away much. I knew Coach Barry was going to be at this next match, but hearing her call him 'dad' right in front of me had me feeling a whole new wave of guilt when remembering her soft, curvy body underneath mine last night before she came to her senses. For the both of us.

"Yep. Okay. Yeah. Yeah. Sounds good. Okay, see you soon. Bye." Meredith hung up the phone, looking down at it for a moment before tucking it securely back into her purse.

"They're at the hotel. We should be there in ten."

"They?"

Yeah," Meredith turned to me, looking me in the eye for the first time since last night, "Rhett and Ava came too."

*Great.* My attention was shot to hell and now I'd have a crowd sitting in the front row, all the people that were counting on me the most other than my younger sisters. I let out a slow breath through my nose, trying to calm my nerves.

"Nico, you okay?" Meredith glanced up at me, her voice sounding like she wasn't sure whether she wanted the real answer or the bullshit pleasantry one.

"Yeah, all good." I went for the latter. I wasn't okay but I would be. I'd get my head back where it belonged: in the ring. Just as soon as I got out of this tight confined space with this mercurial, gorgeous redhead whose lips I could still taste on my own.

"Nico! Looking good, boy. Feeling another W on the board tonight?" Coach pulled me into a quick hug before slapping my back, his bald head just at my chin. The guy had never been much of a legend in the ring, but he'd trained the best. Rhett just gave me a chin nod, his usual form of acknowledgement.

"Nico, I hope you've been getting some rest between

matches. This schedule is grueling but Meredith seems like she has it all under control." Ava gave me her megawatt smile and I didn't miss the way Rhett tensed even though Ava never looked at anyone the way she looked at him. She gave me a hug but I kept my hands at my sides. No way was I going to risk an unnecessary punch from Rhett before my match.

"Meredith's been great." I don't look at her when I say it. There's so much more to my words that only she knows but it's the closest thing I'll get to ending whatever last night was.

"The training center isn't too far from here. Why don't you get checked in and then we can head out in about an hour? Give the girls a break from the fighting." Coach Barry winked at me but there was a tension pulling at the soft lines in his face, almost like he was nervous. I noticed that he and Meredith didn't hug and barely spoke.

We checked in at the front desk, Meredith handling all of the logistics as per usual. She turned to hand me a set of key cards and nearly ran into my chest because I had been standing so close. I took a breath and backed up, but not before I could smell the sweet peachy scent of her hair.

"Two rooms this time," Meredith handed me the cards, a small smile on her face.

"I kinda liked having a roommate." I kept my voice light, wanting to break some of the tension. She smiled briefly before her stoic expression settled back over her face and she left me to go talk to Ava.

"Hey," Rhett gripped the back of my neck in his hand as he guided me toward the hotel elevators. We got into an elevator and I used my key card to get to the right floor.

"How long has it been?" Rhett leaned against the inside

of the elevator cab, his eyes squinted slightly as he studied me.

"Since what?"

"You got laid."

My surprised expression reflected back at me in the glass of the elevator walls and I blinked a few times before saying anything. "Why do you care?" Rhett smirked before looking down at his boots and then back up at me, "You're wound so tight I think you might snap in half. Fucking and fighting go hand in hand. You got a girlfriend we can fly out?"

The elevator door pinged open and I hurried to get out. But Rhett was close behind me. I found my room and set my suitcase on the bed, still not answering his question.

"Nico?" Rhett blocked me in the hallway and I ran my hand through my hair. This guy was supposed to teach me my combinations and yell at me in the corner of the ring between fights. Not ask me about my sex life.

"No girlfriend." I managed to grit out and Rhett nodded slowly.

"Good. That's good. More of a distraction." I swallowed hard past the lump in my throat that had me thinking of Meredith. "You need to find another way, okay? This is no joke. As your coach, I'm telling you. Can you manage or do you need a wingman?" Rhett was standing in front of me with his arms across his chest, always in a casual fighting stance. I let out a nervous laugh.

"A wingman?" My nervous laugh turned into a real one at the thought of Rhett actually trying to help me pick up women.

"Look," Rhett put up his hands in mock surrender, "I'm asking if you can handle this. Or if you need some...help."

"I can handle it." My words were rushed as I forced an

end to this awkward conversation. Rhett nodded at me but he didn't look fully convinced.

"Good. Now get changed so we can spar a bit. Gotta make sure you haven't lost everything I've taught you already. Meet you in the lobby in five."

By the time I got to the gym, my mind was crowded with Meredith. Her red hair and glassy eyes, the way she'd softened underneath me until she came to her senses and froze completely. That felt like shit. Like I'd done something wrong which I knew I had but that didn't mean I'd wanted it to stop. Far from it. And now Rhett had to go and talk about my sex life and remind me of how important sex was before a fight and that just made me want her all the more. There was no way I could just find some random girl like the women at the club back in Philadelphia. I wanted sex like any other guy, but I didn't want it that way.

"Focus, Chavez! Jesus." Rhett dropped his hands by his sides, his brow furrowed. "You're fighting Monroe tonight and he's good. Has as much energy as you, but he's a mean fucker. An advantage you don't have."

I stared back at Rhett. He was bulkier than me but I had a few inches on him. "I can be mean."

Rhett laughed and the sound was dark, mocking. "No Chavez, you can't. You've got agility and adrenaline and energy but you don't have *mean*. You fight to move. Not to kill."

"You don't know shit." The words were out of my mouth before I could stop them. Part of me knew Rhett was right. I wasn't the typical brawling brute. I wasn't as hard around the edges as him or maybe as my upcoming opponent Monroe. But I was fighting for survival too. For a chance at freedom and financial security. For a way out of the shithole I'd grown up in. I was quiet about it, polite even. But that streak was in me. It was in all of us. No completely sane person would put themselves between those ropes otherwise.

"You want to be mean?" Rhett spit on the mat before assuming a fighting stance again. "Then be fucking mean, Chavez. Right now." I bolted straight at him, the frustration that I kept deep within me coming full force to the surface. I saw a deep flash of red before I realized that Rhett had hit the mat below my feet, a large gash under his chin. He was smiling. Any other person would be screaming or in tears. I didn't smile in return as I walked backwards to the center of the ring, keeping eye contact with him the entire time.

"Get up." My tone was clear. I was done being looked at as the polite, head-nodding underdog. Rhett didn't get to tell me who to have sex with or that I wasn't mean.

"I don't know what's gotten into you," Rhett lifted himself up, his breath rising heavily, "but don't lose it." I didn't say anything in response and once Rhett was back in position I rushed him again, putting every ounce of energy I had into each blow.

"Woah, woah, son! Save it for tonight." I dropped my fists at the sound of Coach Barry's voice as he stood outside of the ring, his expression a mixture of pride and worry. I glanced away from him quickly, still feeling guilty about my thoughts of Meredith.

"Looks like our golden boy does have a darkside after all." Rhett shrugged, a satisfied grin still on his face.

"Shut up." I hopped out of the ring, heading into the locker room. It was like Rhett's taunting had broken some-thing loose deep inside of me. I didn't want to be mean. I wanted to be free, to be loved, to be protected. But if being mean in the ring would get me to that place of freedom faster, then I'd be as nasty as the rest of them.

## 30

## MEREDITH

Something was definitely off. Nico didn't smile at me or even look in my direction in his pre-fight prepping room. My dad and Rhett were busy taping his hands, giving him the inside scoop on his opponent tonight, Jason Monroe, while Ava chatted in my ear about all the updates happening at the gym. I liked Ava a lot but was hardly listening to her. I was too distracted by the aggravated look on Nico's face. His dimple was miles away. I'd really come to like that dimple.

"Sorry, I'm sure I'm boring you," Ava laughed and I smiled at her, realizing that I'd totally spaced out for the last several minutes. "Do you like the fights? I found them really overwhelming in the beginning but then they grew on me. The underground ones aren't as glamorous as this."

"Yeah, they're fine. Kinda like a concert." I glanced down at my phone, hoping for a text from Toni as I used her comparison as if it were my own. The fights were fine. This gig was fine. I was fine. But Nico? Nico was not fine. I had to remind myself that I barely knew the guy and that I shouldn't be acting like I could accurately read his mood from across a room. Still, a sense of unease blossomed in my stomach and I nervously sipped from a bottle of water, my mouth feeling too dry from nerves.

"Why don't you two head on out, the fight should be starting in thirty." Ava gently grabbed my arm and we made our way through the backstage hallways until we met an usher who took us to our seats. Front and center. The arena was even more packed tonight than the last one.

"So," Ava smoothed the bottom of her dress as she took her seat, her smile bright, "how's Nico getting along? I know these tours can be pretty overwhelming from what I've heard. He seems to be handling it well?"

"I think so," my voice trailed off as I battled between wanting to be honest and wanting this conversation to end.

"Good, that's good." Ava's voice was kind but tentative. "I think we've secured a tour manager for him for the second half. Her name is Amelia, I think you'd really like her. Both of her brother's are fighters and her dad is a coach so she kind of grew up in this world like you."

"I didn't grow up with this." My tone was rude. Demeaning. As if *this* was the last place I wanted to be. And it had been, a mere few weeks ago. But now, a wave of jealousy crashed through me at the thought of this *Amelia* taking my place, even though it had always been abundantly clear about how temporary this whole thing was.

"Right, sorry. I didn't mean--"

"It's fine, Ava. No big deal. I just barely knew my dad growing up, that's all." My facade was back up and in full force. I hated how quickly I reverted to that place but it was my defense mechanism. Besides, it was for the better. In a few months, I'd be back on campus, hundreds of miles away from this fighting world and my dad...and Nico. Better to make it a clean break and not muddy the waters with concerns about whether Nico was off tonight or not. He had a job to do and that was to win in the ring. I was simply here to get him from point A to point B. And more importantly, to stay as far away from Hewitt as possible.

The lights started to dim and luckily Ava didn't say anything else. I would've ended up just continuing to be mean to her and I didn't want that. I liked Ava. She was smart and beautiful and insanely helpful. And here I was, being my bitchy self. But it was easier that way. The less connections I made, the easier it would be when all of this was over.

"Good evening," the announcer purred into the microphone, sending the audience into overdrive at the realization that the match was officially starting, "we have two new fighters tonight, both ready to fight hard in order to make a name for themselves. Our first fighter this evening is brand new to the circuit. From what I've been told, he has the energy, stamina, and grace of an Olympian. Let's see if his athleticism will be enough for him tonight..." my heart started to thunder in my chest, knowing that Nico was going to be announced first based on the MCs's description alone, "please give a warm and riotous welcome to Nico Chavez!" The crowd erupted in a mix of welcoming screams and deafening boos. What would it feel like to come into an arena packed to the brim with half of its occupants wanting you to get knocked out cold? I shuddered at the thought of it and turned slightly in my seat to try and put a face to all the people that were hoping Nico would lose tonight.

"It's always like that for the newer fighters." Ava didn't look at me when she spoke, keeping her gaze fixed on the lit up ring but somehow still knowing how much the booing bothered me. I hated that she could read me so clearly and I hoped it didn't look like I had any feelings for Nico. Because

I didn't. He was hot and sexy and boyishly charming but that was it, right?

But when I saw him enter the ring, my string of thoughts evaporated. He was tall and glowing, his olive skin looking warm under the spotlights and his dark eyes glaring out at the crowd. I silently begged for him to find me and smile the same way he had the other night, with that damn dimple appearing deep in his cheek. But he didn't. He simply glowered. The angst looked foreign on his face, out of place. A small chill crept up my spine. Something was one hundred percent most definitely wrong and I hated that I didn't know what it was.

"And next, my good friends..." The announcer cooed again, loving the mix of emotion from tonight's audience, "we can't leave Mr. Chavez in this ring all by himself now can we?" The audience yelled out incoherent responses as the announcer waited for the noise to lower enough so that he could speak again, "Tonight, we have a former street fighter. A criminal. A renegade. A young man you wouldn't want to meet in a dark alley alone..." I fidgeted in my seat at the unsavory description of the opponent that would soon be mere feet from Nico. "Ladies and gentlemen, I give you, Jason Monroe!" The screams ratched even higher and I resisted the urge to cover my ears. I glanced over to Ava to see that she had and she smiled back sheepishly. I let out a little laugh, not that anyone could hear it. But the laughter died on my lips when I saw Monroe enter the ring. He was strong and squat. His skin was pale like mine and freckles dotted his upper shoulders, neck, and face. He looked Irish. And he looked scary as fuck. My gaze switched to Nico whose face had grown even angrier than when he'd been announced. Both men made their way to their respective corners and I unsuccessfully willed one last time that Nico would look my way. We were so close, I could even hit him with a baseball and my aim was horrid. We were so close but so far away. His eyes were laser-focused and dark, blocking out everything except Monroe. There was something so foreign and so angry in Nico's eyes that I closed mine shut when the loud clang of the bell rang out. I didn't want to watch. Not like this. Not when I knew that whatever was going on with Nico went way beyond just wanting to fight and win. It was like a switch had gone off.

"Something's wrong." The words were a rough whisper but Ava still heard me. She cocked her head to the side, glancing between me and the ring.

"With Nico. Something's wrong."

"Like physically? Is he hurt?" Ava craned her neck, trying to study Nico for any broken ribs or gashes that could be affecting his movements but there were none. His limbs were swift, his movements solid, but he and Monroe were fighting so tightly it was hard to distinguish one body from the other.

"He's not hurt. He's just..." I stopped talking, not sure how to explain it without looking like I had a big fat crush on him. Which I was still convincing myself that I didn't. "He's just not himself." As the words left my mouth, Monroe hit the floor with a reverberating thud, Nico standing over him like a Greek gladiator. The announcer began to move in, the crowd going wild, when Nico bent down low and threw a forceful jab at Monroe's jaw. I gripped the armrests of my seat as the crowd bellowed out in a mixture of fury and excitement. I barely knew the rules of this sport, this deadly game, but even I knew that you don't punch your opponent once they're already on the mat and the round has been called. Ava and I exchanged a

nervous glance as my dad began yelling from the edge of
the ring, Rhett having to keep him from slipping in through
the ropes.

"I need to talk to him," I started to get up from my seat,
Ava resting a hand on my forearm.

"Meredith, I'm not sure that's a good--"

"Ava, please." She stared at me for a moment, the entire
arena in overdrive as Monroe was dragged back to his
corner, his coach screaming so hard that the veins in his
neck looked like they were going to pop right out. We made
our way from the first row over to the corner where Rhett
and my dad were arguing. I'd never seen my dad this angry
in my entire life. I'd barely ever seen him at all.

"Meredith!" He turned to me, his face red and his lips
sputtering, "What the hell are you two doing? Go sit down."
I physically jerked back, feeling like a young child being
chastised by her father.

"I need to talk to him." My voice was cold, detached. But
my legs were shaking like a leaf in the wind.

"What?" My dad looked like a crazed animal, "Meredith,
it's not in your job description to manage what he does in
the ring. That's our job. And clearly we're not doing a very
good job of it right now." He jabbed his thumb at Rhett who
stroked his jaw thoughtfully, looking like he was trying to
decide whether or not to remain the calm one or hop into
the ring himself and beat Nico up. Before anyone could do
anything else, the announcer called a timeout, requested by
Monroe's team. A ref in the ring squatted down, his head
still above us.

"It's either going to be a null round or disqualification."
My dad raised his arms in anger. "Don't fight me on this,
Barry. The rules are the rules. This isn't the underground."
My dad blabbered out an incoherent string of curse words

before putting his hands on his hips and hanging his head low.

Ava moved closer to Rhett, "What now?"

"Back to the prepping room. Before he does something else stupid." I raised my eyebrows at Rhett's rude tone, suddenly wondering if he or my dad were somehow the root of all this. Nico had been fine before they got here. What had they done or said to him between when I'd seen Nico at the hotel and now? It didn't make sense.

Ava and I started following Rhett and my dad towards the back when Rhett turned around to face us. "Not you two. Head back front row until the decision is called. We don't need it looking like our team is assuming a disqualification already." Ava nodded and I crossed my arms over my chest. "I don't take orders from you."

"Meredith I think--" Ava tried to interject, always the mediator. But I wasn't in a mood to be mediated.

"Right now, you do. If you want to support Nico, the best thing you can do is show your solidarity from the front row." He spit out at me, using Nico like a weapon. I didn't like that one bit. I saw what Ava saw in Rhett. He was hot as hell, masculine and strong, a no bullshit kind of man. But right now, at this moment, he was being an ass. I rolled my eyes and headed back toward the front row, praying that this fight would resume soon so all the drama could be over. We were hardly twenty minutes into this thing.

It felt like forever before the announcer re-emerged into the ring. The audience was as restless as I felt. I kept crossing and uncrossing my limbs, first my arms and then my legs. Both fighters were still backstage and out of sight. It was like the arena was holding in one, huge collective breath as they waited to hear the fate of this long awaited night that might be cut way too short.

"My dear friends, I am afraid--" the announcer was cut short by the most visceral slew of boos from the crowd. The noise was so painful, that I could feel it pierce within my chest as if my own lungs were two balloons being popped with a needle. "The Monroe team has decided that the post round blow by Nico Chavez is grounds for disqualification from this match. Neither fighter will take a win or a loss this evening. They will reconvene here in two days time and your tickets will still be valid--" before the announcer could continue with technicalities, screams and shouts punctured the air, leaving no room for rescheduling details.

"Ladies, come with me. Now please." Our usher reappeared, a stressed look on his face. Ava and I glanced between one another without saying another word. When we went outside, a black car was already waiting for us and I briefly wondered who had arranged it for us since it wasn't me this time.

"Rhett ordered the car." Ava glanced at me quickly before glancing back down at her phone as we slid into the backseat. "The boys are back at the hotel." The way she said *the boys* made it feel like we were all part of this together. But we weren't. I was temporary. *Amelia* would be replacing me soon.

When we got to the hotel I wasn't sure what to do. I had my own room with my own key. I could go back there and put on a movie. Maybe call Toni and see what was keeping her so busy that she couldn't respond to my texts throughout this rather disastrous evening. Ava shifted in her heels, feeling the same sense of awkwardness after all of the chaos of the arena.

"I, uh, should probably go check on Rhett and--"

"Yeah, yeah totally. Go." I smiled at her and she faltered for a moment before responding.

"Do you want to come up?"

"What? No, I'm good. I'll head to my room. I need to see how the reschedule affects our travel dates anyway."

"Okay. Get some rest, Meredith. I'm sure it'll all blow over in a few days." Ava left and headed toward the elevator bay. I stayed back, not wanting to follow just after her. There was literally nothing more awkward than going in the same direction as someone after you'd just said goodbye to. I loitered in the elegant hotel lobby for a few moments before calling Toni.

"Hey! Sorry, Red. I was out tonight. On a date actually." Toni's friendly voice made me feel a little better.

"A date?! Wait, what? With who?"

"Ugh, who cares. It was a disaster. I'm never going to see him again. Tell me about your night, I couldn't tell what was going on from your texts."

"It was a disaster too. Like, really bad."

"What happened?"

I started walking toward the bay of elevators but just before I launched into the saga that was this evening I heard a little ping and glanced down at my phone.

UNKNOWN @ 10:23 PM: Hey, you make it back okay?

MY HEART STARTED to pound in my chest. My first instinct was that the text was possibly Hewitt on a burner phone or a new number. But how would he know about me getting back to the hotel?

"Um, Earth to Meredith? Are you still there?" Toni's voice sounded small from the speaker in my phone, held a few inches from my ear as I stared back at those three little blinking dots across my text screen.

"Hey, uh, Toni let me call you back. Sorry, in an elevator." I hung up distractedly and rode the elevator the rest of the way to my floor, replying to the mystery text and getting a response.

MEREDITH @ 10:25 PM: Who is this?

UNKNOWN @ 10:26 PM: It's Nico.

I PAUSED LOOKING DOWN at the screen and seeing his name there. I made the decision so quickly it was like not making one at all. Instead of turning left toward my room, I turned right. Toward his.

## 31

## NICO

I stared down at my phone, waiting for Meredith to respond. The three text dots kept appearing and disappearing before disappearing for good. I groaned and tossed the phone on my bed. I hated that I'd let Rhett get to me tonight. First with his bullshit about me needing to get laid and then about me not being *mean* enough. Not having what it takes. It definitely made sense why Rhett could only fight in the underground. There's no way he'd last a minute on these tours without breaking the rules. I hung my head in my hands, hoping this would all blow over soon and that I wouldn't have to tell my sisters that something stupid I'd done in a moment of frustration had fucked up my entire contract. Before I could stress anymore about my contract terms, a soft knock sounded at my hotel room door. *Damn, the room service here was fast.* I'd ordered my dinner only ten minutes ago.

I went to the door and quickly undid the latch.

"Meredith?"

"Hi," her voice trailed off as she looked me up and down,

staring a moment too long at my bare chest. I'd already changed into joggers for bed after a shower. I glanced up and down the hallway to check that she was alone.

"I'm alone, Nico."

"Just checking."

"Are you going to let me in?" A faint smirk pulled at her lips, her pretty face looking perfect but tired. I didn't respond but I opened the door wider and she ducked in under my arm. She stood in the middle of the hotel living room area, looking like she had something to say.

"Meredith, I'm glad you're back safe and I'm sorry about tonight, I am, but I really don't want to talk--"

"Something really bad happened to me," she cut me off, tilting her head and I started to move toward her in concern, "not tonight. A few months ago. Something really bad happened to me a few months ago and to other people too and I don't talk about it. I won't ever talk about it. But," she started pacing slowly, glancing up at me between steps, "but it changed me. It made me...mean. Cold, bitchy. I've been called every name in the book since it happened." She laughed but the sound was sad. I didn't move. I just stood still a few feet from the front door, waiting to see what she'd say next.

"I don't need to know what happened to you, but something triggered it tonight. Something made you mean. And you're not like that, Nico. That's not who you are and you don't need to be that way or use anything painful from your past in order to be a good fighter."

Meredith stared at me for a moment longer and I didn't know what to say. It was the most words she'd ever spoken to me at once and I couldn't believe how well she'd been able to read me. I took in a few deep breaths before responding.

"If I ask you what happened to you...you won't tell me?"

Meredith stared right at me, her shoulders straightening, "No."

I nodded, not happy with her response but not wanting to push her. "Are you okay now?"

Meredith tilted her head to the side and licked her bottom lip, a thoughtful look settling over her face. "I don't know...but right now, at this exact moment, I feel pretty good." Before I could respond, there was another knock at my door. Meredith's eyes went wide, glancing between me and the door.

"Room service." Meredith nodded and settled in on the couch. I didn't stop looking at her as I made my way to the door, fearful that she'd try to leap up and run out after her confession. I mean, it made sense. The way she'd go from hot to cold, opened up to completely closed off. And I never knew what triggered it or when to expect the shifts. But I'd learn. I'd make it my job to know.

"You hungry?" I set the pizza down on the oversized coffee table and removed the ridiculously formal silver domed cover.

"Is pizza your primary food group?" I smirked at Meredith before wolfing down a piece, using a linen hotel napkin to wipe my face.

"Normally, no. I'm actually not a terrible cook, but my sister usually makes dinner for us and she's damn good." I took another piece, Meredith's eyes fixated on each of my movements. It was hot, like she was tracking me.

"Eat a piece before I--"

"Finish the whole thing?" She lifted an eyebrow at me and I smiled back as she daintily took the smallest piece.

We talked until we finished the pizza, Meredith only eating two pieces. When she got up to excuse herself, I cleaned up and settled back on the couch. My hands were itching to run through her hair, over her skin. I wanted to taste her again. But I wasn't about to let what happened last time happen again. She needed to either be in or out. Even if it was just for tonight. And more than anything, even more than wishing I could take back my idiotic behavior in the ring today, I wished that she'd be in.

Meredith came to the living room but didn't sit down. She had her hands in jeans pockets and rocked lightly back and forth on her feet. She looked like she was itching to leave. The exact opposite of what I wanted to see from her.

"Well, I better go. Hopefully the rematch will get scheduled for tomorrow." I didn't respond. Instead, I settled further into the couch, my legs spread casually and my arm draped over the back. I was still learning to read this girl, but I could see it in her face. The look that she didn't want to leave. At least not yet.

She started to turn away and I spoke up, "So, you said something bad happened to you? And I'm guessing that's why you close off and shut down randomly, out of nowhere. And I get it. I'm not saying I can relate to whatever happened to you, but you were right when you said that I've been through some shit. In my past." She turned back toward me, not moving closer but also not moving away.

"My entire youth has been spent trying, desperately hoping to get away from the shitty hand I'd been dealt. All I do is worry or work or feel guilty about not worrying or working for my sisters' sake," I leaned forward, resting my forearms on my knees and staring up at Meredith, her pale eyes locked on mine, "but when I'm around you, I forget about all of that. I become selfish. I want to feel good. Really good. Like all that other shit doesn't exist. Do you feel that too?" My voice became deeper and more hoarse, my words both confident and pleading. Meredith swallowed hard, her delicate neck working past the emotion she was feeling.

"Yes." Her response was nothing more than a whisper. And while that small little word had me wanting to leap up from the couch and pull her onto my lap, I didn't. If we were going to try this again, she was going to have to come to me.

"Well then, stop running and let me make you feel good." I raised my eyebrows at her, throwing down a challenge. I leaned back slowly against the couch, draping my arm again over the back. Meredith squinted her eyes at me, but a smirk pulled at her lips. *That's my girl.*

She walked over slowly, setting her purse down on the ground and gently straddling over my thighs. She grabbed my shoulders for support and I lightly rested my hands on her small waist, guiding her closer to me. She stared at my lips for what felt like forever, before looking up at me and then moving closer, her face just half an inch from mine.

"Kiss me, Meredith."

Her lips locked onto mine, surprisingly forceful and desperate as I dragged my hands up into her thick hair, grabbing the back of her head so I could keep her close. She tasted just as good as before, maybe even better, as soft mewling noises escaped her lips and my tongue explored her mouth. She was soft and strong and fire and ice, all in one. The sensation of her this close to me almost burned it felt so fucking good.

I moved my hand up under her shirt, going more slowly than I'd like. I couldn't risk losing her like last time. She had to stay here, in the present, with me the entire time. I cupped her left breast and then her right, freeing each from the bra cup and seeing how full and perfect her breasts felt in my palms. I twisted her nipple gently and she groaned, grinding her hips harder against mine.

Meredith leaned back, breaking our kiss, and pulled off her shirt and bra. I stared at her, dragging my tanned calloused hands over her smooth, pale skin. I took my hand further south, my thumb covering the zipper of her jeans.

"Are you with me?" My words were strangled, my desire for her body making it hard for me to control myself but I wouldn't have her if she was off somewhere else, thinking of the past.

"Yes." Meredith nodded fervently, placing her small delicate hand over mine and guiding me to unzip her jeans. The look in her eyes was electric. I unzipped her jeans and she placed her palms on the back of the couch for leverage so I could pull them down her legs. She settled back on my lap, her lace underwear and the material of my joggers the only thing separating us. Without saying anything, Meredith dragged her palm over my pants, rubbing me through the fabric in a way that felt so good I let out a loud groan. She kept repeating the movement, speeding up the pace.

"Jesus, Meredith, you're killing me." I heard her laugh and the sound sent another jolt of pleasure down my back. I grabbed her wrist to stop her movement and without shifting her off of my lap, I arched up off the couch and slid my joggers down my legs. Before I could stop her, she grabbed me in her hand and moved her lace panties to the slide, placing me at her entrance.

"You make me feel good," Meredith rushed out, her voice breathy as she slid me inside of her, a mixture of pleasure and pain taking over her face, "really, really good." I grabbed her hips and thrust myself fully inside of her, trying to take it slow but finding it nearly impossible to fully control myself. I started to move my hips but Meredith placed her palm on my chest and looked up into my eyes.

"Give me a sec," she wiggled on top of me and I stayed still as marble, allowing her to get comfortable with me fully inside of her. It was sexy and adorable and intoxicating watching her feel her own body as she explored mine. After a few moments she nodded at me and I started to move, slowly at first and then faster. The feeling was heady. It rivaled the feeling I got in the ring, and as our rhythm increased, her head tossing back and her breasts bouncing in my face, I decided it was even better. Better than any high I'd ever experienced in the ring.

I lost myself in her body, hands roaming, course kisses interjecting our movements as we strained against the pleasure building up inside of us. Meredith was the first to break.

"Nico, I'm close." She rested her head in the crook of my neck, the sounds of her orgasm right at my ear. It drove me towards my own and I gripped her waist desperately as I came, almost like I was worried that once this part ended she'd run away.

"Fuck, Meredith. You're perfect." I kissed the side of her neck, her skin smelling sweet and tasting salty with sweat. Her forehead rested on my shoulder, both of us unable to move for the moment. Finally she pushed herself off of me, standing on shaky legs and pulling her lace underwear back in place.

Meredith started to pick up her discarded clothes slowly but I didn't move. I tracked her like a hawk, looking for any signs that I'd lost her. That she wasn't still here, with me, in the present place where everything felt good and right.

"You're still here?" She held her clothes to her chest, her

cheeks rosy and her red hair a wild, beautiful mane around her face.

"I'm still here." She smiled warmly at me, and I knew she was telling the truth. She leaned over and kissed me lightly before heading off toward the bathroom.

## 32

## MEREDITH

I felt a buzzing vibration. I couldn't tell if it was the satisfaction in my own, relaxed limbs or something else. Finally, the vibration became so strong that I rubbed the heels of the palms to my eyes, willing it away. But it didn't stop.

"Is that your phone or mine?" Nico's masculine and groggy voice caused me to move from half-awake to fully, cold-water-splashed-on-my face awake. I glanced over at the hotel nightstand and saw my phone vibrating, my dad's name flashing across the screen.

"Meredith! It's nearly 10:00 A.M. and I can't get a hold of Nico. Can you find out where he is?" My dad's voice was loud enough to be heard through the phone and Nico's dimple came out in all of its glory as we stifled an awkward laugh.

"Um, yeah one sec. I'll text him." I grinned at Nico and he sat up straighter in bed, his thick hair sticking out in every direction. He tried to grab me but I shoved him away, knowing I wouldn't be able to restrain my laughter if he got to me.

"He just woke up, slept in. All good." My dad grumbled something else I couldn't hear and I hopped out of bed.

"Well, good. I started to worry that he'd gone on a bender or ended up with some hooker last night." I blinked rapidly at his statement, glancing back at Nico who had a "what's wrong" look on his face that I shoved away with my hand, not wanting to relay my dad's assumptions to him.

"Any word on the rematch?"

"Yes, it's tonight. Thank fuck, oh, sorry honey, thank goodness, they aren't dragging this out or turning it into a bigger issue than this. Nico nearly lost his ass with that little stunt."

"What time?" I brushed over my dad's criticism of Nico, wanting to move past the whole thing.

"8:00 P.M. start. Earlier than normal but we'll take it. Go to his room and get him out of bed, we need to take all training precautions today. Make sure he's in a good space."

"Yep, I'm on it." More like, already done but there was no way in hell we'd be telling my dad that. Ever. The thought was an unwelcome one as I stole a glance back at Nico who was getting out of bed, realizing that whatever this was, it would probably go nowhere. I was still the coach's daughter to Nico after all.

"What's up?" Nico walked over, pulling on his joggers and kissing me lightly on the cheek like we did this every morning. I smiled shyly, my cheeks warming.

"Rematch. Tonight at 8:00 P.M. My dad wants to see you soon for training. I'm currently headed toward your hotel room right now to tell you that."

Nico wrapped a strong, long arm around my waist and pulled me flush against him, "Is that right?" He kissed his way up my neck, embarrassingly girly giggles escaping my throat. He was warm, his skin heating mine.

"Hey, Nico, Nico!" I laughed, pushing away at his strong chest but making zero progress. He was a wall of lean muscle. "My dad will probably be here soon. You need to get ready."

Nico stopped kissing me and sighed heavily, a sad smile on his handsome face, "And you need to leave." I nodded in agreement and put on my discarded clothes as I tried to pull my wild hair into a semblance of a ponytail. I opened the hotel room door slowly, looking both ways for signs of anyone from the gym team. When the coast was clear I turned back to Nico who was leaning against the couch.

"See you later?"

"Planning on it." He winked at me and I rolled my eyes even though I loved it. I freaking *loved* it when he winked at me. When his dimple appeared. I left quickly before I said or did anything stupid like admitting out loud just how much I loved those little things about him.

I DIDN'T SEE Nico again until the rematch. I spent the entire day with Ava, moving around flights and hotel accommodations for our next step as well as planning out a few more tour destinations down the line. I hated when Ava would mention that Amelia could handle this tour stop or that PR engagement. I nodded quietly but it only served to remind me that I would be gone in three months. A temporary blip on the radar. Nico would still be touring. Fighting. Likely winning. And I'd be back in sunny California, sitting in an auditorium-sized classroom thinking about him.

Ava and I took our front row seats, my nerves strung out at the thought of seeing Nico again even though we'd be separated by the ring. Flashes of the previous night crossed my mind, Nico's lips and hands. His dimple and his smirk being replaced by a serious look of pleasure and how his brows furrowed and his throat growled when he came. I cleared my throat at the hot thoughts, hoping Ava couldn't read exactly what was going through my mind. When I glanced at her, Ava smiled sweetly in return, no suspicion on her pretty face.

The crowd was even rowdier this evening with the pent up energy of the rematch.

When Nico came out into the ring, the crowd swelled to the seams with a discordant mixture of screams and boos. His dark olive skin glowed warm under the lights and it reminded me of how warm it felt to be held by him. How hot and electric his touch was on my icy skin.

"He looks good tonight, more himself. Don't you think?" Ava talked loudly but it sounded more like a whisper over the noise in the stadium. I nodded my head in agreement, distracted by Nico's humble smile as he looked out at the crowd, acknowledging their frustration but promising a fair match this time.

When his opponent emerged, the noise swelled again and I stared at Nico, worriedly expecting some sort of shift in his demeanor. The two fighters stood several paces apart, feet firmly planted on the mat. Right when it seemed that round one was about to start, Nico started heading toward his opponent and my heart rate spiked. *No, no, no Nico! Don't do anything stupid. This isn't you.*

Nico stopped a foot from his opponent and stuck out his hand. An olive branch. His opponent stared down at it, wary at first, and the crowd went wild. But Nico didn't look at the crowd. It was almost as if they didn't exist at this moment. He stood patiently, calmly, a pleasant but unreadable expression on his face. Finally his opponent took his hand heavily, giving it a quick masculine shake before letting go.

"Well, ladies and gentlemen, looks like sportsmanship does still exist. Let the rematch begin!" Nico bounced lightly on his calves, not making the first move toward the center of the ring. I felt like I was holding my breath, floating deeper and deeper under the surface of the water as I waited for someone to make the first move. Finally, his opponent moved in on him, getting a few jabs to Nico's side before Nico went on the offensive. His movements were stiff and strong, not lingering any longer than necessary. He won the first two rounds but both fighters were at the top of their game, playing smart and aggressive.

After another hour, Nico claimed the final round, the crowd going wild as the announcer raised his long tanned arm high above his head and photographers circled the ring, bright lights blinding the surrounding area. Nico smiled, but his face remained stoic. He congratulated his opponent in his respective corner before leaving the ring and slipped out under the rope deftly. I lost sight of him for a moment and started to move toward the aisle against the crowd when I felt a soft grip around my upper arm.

"Nico?" My voice was shocked and breathless as his tall, sweaty body towered over mine.

"We need to talk, Meredith. I feel good, really good, and I know it's because of you."

My heart sang in my chest but I looked around me warily as I noticed various photographers snapping photos, not to mention the surprised but knowing look on Ava's face as she stood a few feet away, watching us.

"You want to talk...now? As in right now? Can't we talk about this in the car--"

"I want this to work. For us to work. And I don't feel like

we shouldn't try just because your dad is my coach. I mean, we can talk to him, explain our situation. Whatever it is, Meredith, that's holding you back, just tell me and I'll fix it, I'll make it right--"

"It's not my dad, Nico."

"Okay, then what is it?"

My entire body froze like lead weights had replaced my legs and my arms had been tethered to my sides. I felt all the blood drain from my face as I stared just beyond Nico's broad shoulder. My voice was hoarse as I managed to whisper the name I hated to speak aloud, the name that wasn't only on my tongue but was in my line of sight, "It's Hewitt."

## 33

# MEREDITH

"**M**eredith, what's wrong? Who's Hewitt?" Nico placed his large warm palms on my shoulders, his face concerned. But his voice sounded like it was somewhere far away. Like he was on the warm sand of a beach and I was floating out to sea, my arms failing me, my voice gone. Just floating.

"Nico, interviews. Let's go. Nice work tonight." My dad came over and tapped Nico's back as photographers started to move into our bubble. The commotion tore us apart, Nico's gaze not leaving my face until he was forced to by distance.

And then it was just us. The *us* that I hated. The *us* that had changed how I saw life, how I saw myself. Hewitt's sandy hair was longer than he usually kept it, his face a bit wild and unkempt. His eyes were fixated on mine and once he realized that I had no place to run, no other distractions to fall back to, he nodded his head toward the right indicating for me to meet him. Again I felt like I was submerged in water, my limbs light and heavy at the same time, moving of their own volition toward Hewitt. If he was here, if he'd managed to find me, then it must be bad. Really bad. Our last phone call flashed through my memory as I picked my way through the thick crowd.

"DON'T HANG UP. *I know I put you in a shit position. I shouldn't have done that. But I miss you...*"

"*I need one more favor. I have a delivery due and the cops are onto me. Someone snitched. Probably that fucker Truman. I have to lay low. But these guys, my supplier, they don't fuck around...*"

"*Listen, Meredith. You don't get to just say 'no.' You were there. You saw him die and you didn't do anything. You're just as guilty as me...*"

"*Your word against mine, Meredith. Your word against mine, and you're the one who got caught trying to sell drugs on campus. Who do you think the cops will believe, Meredith?*"

I PULLED open the heavy metal door, drowning out the noise from the arena. I felt cold, goosebumps breaking out over my arms and down my back. Nico's warmth seemed like it was thousands of miles away. I found Hewitt leaning against the wall, fidgeting with his phone. He looked thinner, less healthy, and his movements were jerky. He was nervous.

"Meredith." His tone was rushed like we didn't have much time but he was trying to play cool like he still had the upper hand. Hewitt always wanted to have the upper hand. "Don't leave. Don't tell me to go away. You *need* to hear what I'm about to tell you." Something in his eyes was genuine, but it wasn't a concern for me. It was fear. True, unadulterated fear. I didn't respond but I didn't leave either. Hewitt looked down at the ground before continuing, "I got caught.

Dealing. The cops put the pieces together. I'm going to have to testify. My lawyers, they..." he paused and swallowed hard, "they said I have to blame the dealers. I have to say that they threatened my life...our lives...if we didn't do what we did. I'll be a marked man but at least I won't be in jail. It's our only shot." He moved closer to me and lifted his hand toward my face. I flinched away instinctively like he was about to hit me.

"Why," I gathered myself, my hands shaking, "why do you keep talking about this like it has anything to do with me? You threatened me to sell those drugs, Hewitt. You did. I've never even talked to these dealers. I was high one time and I didn't intervene when someone was dying. And that is a guilt I will carry with me forever. But I'm not part of this. You have to let me go. Just please, Hewitt, let me go." My voice broke on the last word, tears flowing without sound from my eyes. I was *begging* the person who had brought me to the darkest part of myself.

"I can't, Meredith." Hewitt slammed his palm against the wall, his jaw grinding in anger. "I can't let you go. You're in this. With me. I'm not going down alone." His eyes turned dark, his body looming over mine. Awareness settled in, cold and heavy like an anchor in my stomach. Pulling me down, deeper into the water's depths.

"If I don't agree with your story you're going to try and take me down, aren't you? You're going to blame me somehow if the court doesn't believe you?"

Hewitt ran his hand through his hair and then moved even closer to me, sucking in all the air around us until I felt like I was really and truly drowning. "It doesn't have to end that way! It doesn't have to, Meredith. Just say exactly what I tell you to when you testify. Listen to my lawyers. They will get us out of this. I'll save you, Meredith. I'll save us. We can be like old times again. It will be good, I promise. You won't have to run anymore. Neither of us will."

My vision started to blur and the hallway seemed like it was tilting back and forth, rocking my body like a ship.

*When you testify...*

*Listen to my lawyers...*

*Lie for me, lie with me, just one more time...*

I felt like I was about to vomit, the tears drying on my cheeks. The rush that I felt within me rose to the surface so violently, it took me by surprise.

"No! Hewitt, no. I will not lie. I got to this place because of lies. Because of you. You are not saving me from anything. You are damning me!"

A shadow crossed over Hewitt's face and I felt warmth. I felt like I was being pulled across the water's surface, breaking through its translucent skin, titling my cheek upward toward the sun.

"I don't know who you are, or what the fuck is going on here, but if you don't back away from her, right the fuck now, I will lay out." Nico's voice was calm on the surface but vibrated with an anger so powerful, so primal, that I felt like it shook the floor beneath us. He was standing right behind me. I couldn't see him, but I could *feel* him.

Hewitt pushed himself off the wall and straightened his shoulders, puffing out his chest. A wicked grin flashed across his face, but the fear never left his eyes. Nico had several inches and pounds of professionally trained muscle on Hewitt. Not to mention that if Hewitt had followed me to this arena, he'd no doubt seen Nico in action during tonight's fight.

"Is that a threat?" Hewitt wouldn't back down. I knew him well enough to know that he wanted to, but his pride had always gotten the best of him.

"It's a promise, *hijo de puta*." Nico growled just above my ear. I'd never heard him use that tone, never heard him speak in Spanish before. It was like a different part of himself was coming through and I knew that if I didn't intervene, we'd have another Nico incident outside of the ring and that was the *last* thing he needed or deserved. I turned around quickly, placing my palm on Nico's bare chest. I looked up at him and he looked like a killer. My warm, smiling, good Nico was going to become a killer for me. I hated myself for it.

"Nico, no. Please." I forgot about Hewitt at my back. About the threats and the cold and the drowning. I was here, just with Nico, on our own island. Surrounded by so much water, just one step in any direction and we'd lose our footing. Lose ourselves. I begged him with my eyes, with the tone of voice, to just stay here with me. Just for one more moment.

"This isn't over, Meredith. I found you so my lawyer can subpoena you. If you don't want to work with me, you're on your own. This was my last offer." I didn't turn around. I wouldn't give Hewitt the satisfaction. I just stood my ground, staring up at Nico. It felt like nothing and yet it felt like forever. Finally, Nico stared down at me, his eyes molten.

"He's gone. He's gone, Meredith." My shoulders sagged at his words, and I hung my head low. Nico finally touched me, his large hand wrapping around my hip as he moved my back up against the wall. As if he just knew I needed the support to keep my legs from buckling. He nestled his head into the crook of my neck, his breathing ragged.

"Talk to me, Meredith. Please." I wanted to reach up and thread my fingers through his hair. I wanted to apologize for making him care so much about me. For dragging him damn near the water's edge and risking what he'd worked so hard for because of the past I'd been desperately running from. I'd brought that past right onto his lap. I wanted to stand up on my tiptoes and kiss him and capture as much of his warmth as I could. But I couldn't. I felt my chest rack with unshed tears and I cried into his chest as he covered me from the view of passersby backstage, just holding me upright until I finally managed to stop.

"What the fuck is this? Nico!" My dad's voice echoed angrily against the concrete hallway. Nico and I both turned in surprise, his hand still on my hip, holding me against the wall. My face red and tearstained.

"Get the fuck off my daughter!" My dad lunged for Nico and my heart rate spiked. He landed a punch in his side and Nico moved to stand between my angry dad and me, absorbing his blows.

"I thought I could trust you! Jesus, Meredith are you alright?" My dad's stare was livid as he looked between the two of us, clearly misreading the entire situation.

"What the fuck, Coach," Rhett growled in a deathly low tone, grabbing my dad's arm before taking in the entire scene. "Nico, walk away. Now." I wanted to scream out. I wanted to tell my dad that he was wrong. That Nico was not the one hurting me. He was the only thing saving me. But my voice was gone, my throat constricting, my eyes darting wildly. I'd ruined everything.

Nico didn't say a word. He put both hands up slowly and backed away a few steps until he turned around and all I could do was stare at his retreating bare back as he made his way down the hallway, a few backstage bystanders whispering to one another.

"Get the fuck out of here. If you say anything to anyone, I'll personally handle you. Understood?" Rhett stared them down and they scrambled off like frightened kittens. My dad rushed over to me, wiping his thumb against my cheek and checking me up and down as if he was looking for signs of injury.

"Meredith, sweetheart, I'm so sorry. I would have never offered you this job role if I'd known that Nico wasn't who I thought he was. I know you'll never forgive me, but I'll do whatever I can to make this right." The lines around his eyes deepened, his face red with anger.

"Dad, please. You don't know what you saw, I'm fine I promise--"

"No. Meredith, don't you dare make excuses for him."

"Enough." Rhett cut in separating us. "This place is too public. Get back to the hotel and deal with this there. I'll go find Nico."

"No, I'm going to find Nico. You take Meredith back to the hotel."

"Coach. I'm not above kicking your ass. I'll do it without regret if you don't leave right the fuck now. Enough damage has already been done. You're not thinking straight since it's your girl. I'm handling this." Rhett shot me a glare like I was to blame. He didn't know but he *knew*. He knew that I was the stain, the problem, not Nico. His glare said it all.

## 34

# NICO

I paced my hotel room restlessly. I flipped my phone in my hand, desperately wanting to call or text Merdith but knowing that I had to lay low right now and let Coach cool off before we could explain what had actually happened. Except even I was asking myself, *what had happened? Who was Hewitt and what was that fucker doing here?* Meredith had looked scared for her life, her icy veneer transparent as she battled to stay standing upright throughout the entire exchange. My hands itched and pulsed to grab that fucker by the throat but Meredith had intervened. The only thing that stopped me were her pleading eyes, telling me without words that if I got in another altercation outside of the ring she'd never not feel guilty about it. She'd never understand that I *wanted* to do it. I wanted to mark her. To protect her. To save her. But from what I knew of Meredith, she wouldn't allow it. That thought had me sinking deeper into my dark and hazy thoughts, hating how helpless I felt confined to my hotel room.

I glanced down at my phone when I realized it was

buzzing. I was hoping it would be Meredith or Rhett with an update but it was my sister Celeste. I took a deep breath before answering, not wanting to give her any cause for concern.

"Hey sis, you burn down the apartment yet?" My tone was teasing but if she could see my expression she'd know it was a front.

"Funny, Nico. No, not yet." She paused briefly and I could hear Maria's TV show blaring in the background. It brought a brief smile to my face. I missed that little stinker. "I just called you to say congratulations on another win! I figured you'd be out partying or something but sounds quiet where you are."

I hung my head and rubbed my eyes, "Thanks, Celeste. Yeah, sometimes I go out after the fights but other times I just need to recover. Reset, you know?" I tried to keep my tone light. I was doing anything other than *recovering* or *resetting* right now. My stomach was in knots and my blood was still boiling from the way Hewitt had spoken to Meredith.

"Yeah, yeah makes sense." Celeste responded in that way that told me she was about to ask for something. She forgot how well I knew her.

"What?" I didn't bother beating around the bush.

"What, what?"

"Celeste, you're about to ask me for something. What is it?" She laughed lightly after an aggravated little noise. Clearly she wasn't as smooth as she thought she was.

"Well, um, I was wondering if maybe, if I can get a sitter for Maria, could I maybe come? To one of your matches? Everyone at school has been talking about how cool it is and I mean, you're my freaking brother. I'd like to come see you kick some ass."

"Celeste! Language."

"Nico, I'm almost seventeen." I slouched down in the chair and laughed silently. She had a point.

"I'll think about it, okay? I promise. I'll need to check with Coach and Meredith--" I cut myself off at my own words. Did I even have my team anymore? The way Coach had looked at me like I was a traitor of the sickest kind. Rhett would sort this out. Help clear the air. He knew it wasn't like what Coach thought he saw. Not even a little bit. *Right?*

"Look, stuff is a little crazy right now," I stood back up to resume pacing and ran a hand through my hair, "but the tour is long so I'm sure there will be a good time for you to come out and see a match."

"Okay! Thanks, Nico. We miss you. Maria! Come say hi to Nico." I heard as Celeste tried to cover the phone speaker and Maria's little feet pounded their way into the kitchen. I could picture her hopping up on the dining room table, excitedly grabbing the phone.

"Nico! Maria doesn't play any fun games with me." Maria's sweet little voice came over the phone and for the first time tonight, I forgot about everything with Meredith. Little kids' purity had a way of cleansing you, even if only for one small moment.

"I'm sure she will if you ask her nicely. Hey, are you doing your schoolwork, helping Celeste around the apartment?"

"Yes, Nico! I'm the best."

"I know you are. My number one."

"When are you coming home?" Her question pained me. The longer I was away from them, the more I could pretend that I was just a young, single fighter trying to make a name for myself. But calls like this reminded me that it wasn't that simple. Nothing in my life was simple. I was making a name for us. For them. A wave of guilt crashed over me as I acknowledged my own recklessness over the past few weeks, things that could have put my contract in jeopardy. It really fucking sucked being responsible sometimes.

"Soon, I promise. I'll have a break in a few weeks I think." I'd have to check with Meredith. She knew my life's schedule better than I did. God, why wouldn't she at least text me? The waiting was killing me.

"Okay, well, I will paint you a picture before you get home! So give me a few days' heads up." Her demanding little tone made me laugh, bringing me back to the happy place that was Maria.

"Deal. I miss you, M. Be nice to Celeste."

"Fineeeee." She hung up the phone after her exaggerated response and I rested my head on my forearm. Finally my phone buzzed once. A text from Rhett.

RHETT @ 10:45: Going to check on Meredith now. Managed to calm Coach down but he still has questions. So do I.

I REPLIED WITH A QUICK 'THANKS' not wanting to elaborate. Fuck, I had questions too. The only one who could piece this story together was Meredith. I wanted to see her. Have her finally open up to me. But even though I hated it, I knew in my gut that she wouldn't. Not yet, not tonight. Not after feeling like she'd brought me to the edge of trouble.

∾

IT WAS PAST MIDNIGHT. No one had reached out to me after Rhett's only text. My limbs were deliciously sore and my body tired, but my mind was electric. Racing. There was no way I could just go to sleep as if this would all blow over in the morning. The thought settled in me, heavy and unwelcome, that Meredith may not even be here in the morning. That the fear, the embarrassment, the unwillingness to share what happened with anyone would drive her away. It was that thought that had me throwing a hoodie over my head and leaving my hotel room in search of her. If she was going to leave, I wouldn't let her do it this way. Not without talking to me first.

## 35

## MEREDITH

I stared at my hands, willing them to stop shaking. Rhett was right. He hadn't been cruel or out of line. He'd just had the balls to say out loud what we'd both been thinking. I hated that it was the truth and that I'd have to act on it. Tomorrow. I had a road ahead of me and the only way out was through. I just hated that that road couldn't include Nico. At least, not right now. And who knew if he'd even want me in several months? Or if he'd want me at all after he found out what I'd been involved in? What I had let Hewitt drag me into? I went into the en suite hotel bathroom and splashed my face with cold water, replaying my earlier interaction with Rhett.

THERE WAS *a knock at my hotel door and while I hoped it was Nico, I knew it wasn't. It was either my dad, who had decided to come back and apologize after being an obstinate, albeit concerned, fool or it was Rhett. I looked through the peephole and saw Rhett standing with his arms over his chest, a tired expres-*

sion on his ruggedly handsome face. I undid the small gold latch and opened the door for him to enter.

"You okay?" Rhett glanced briefly around the room before leveling his gaze at me.

"Uh, no?" I laughed, choking a bit on the bitter sound.

"Are you hurt?" Rhett squinted his eyes, scanning me up and down.

"No, not physically." Rhett just nodded once in response before leaning up against the entry buffet table that served no real purpose other than that of his support at this very moment. His demeanor and his body looked relaxed but the tension in the room was palpable. Neither of us wanted to have this conversation but we both knew we had to have it anyway.

"I don't like to be nosy. I hate that shit. I handle my own and that's that. But you have to understand that Nico is my own. And not just because I'm one of his coaches." This was Rhett's way of telling me how much he cared about Nico and I smiled briefly before my lips returned to a flat, grave line across the lower half of my face.

"I don't want you to think that I don't like you. Or that I think Nico shouldn't like you." Rhett shrugged his shoulders and looked at the ground, almost as if he was talking more to himself than me, "When I told that kid to get laid, I didn't mean with the coach's daughter, Jesus."

"What? You told Nico to get laid...like it was a request?" My voice rose several octaves as I made my way through the sentence. Had I just been a technicality? A way to follow through on a coach's orders? But then Nico's face came back to me, the way he'd gently kept me in the present with his reassuring words and his smile and the sure way that his hands moved over my skin. A guy wouldn't do that if it was just about sex, right?

"Look, clearly he didn't listen to me. He likes you, a lot. And, it's dangerous. It's a huge distraction. Liking any girl as much as he likes you can be a big issue for new fighters on the main circuit." Rhett stopped talking, standing up straighter as he placed both palms flat on the buffet behind him, "But with you--"

"It's even worse." I finished his sentence for him. "I'm not just a distraction, I'm a walking landmine."

"Well, you said it. Not me." Rhett gave me a joking look before his face turned more serious again. "You have some shit you're going through. I don't even want to know what it is. Again, not my business. But you can't keep running from whatever that thing is. You have to deal with it, head on. And leave Nico out of it."

A flush crept over my skin as guilt and concern seeped through my body. I couldn't believe how transparent the whole thing was. My past and what I'd witnessed with Hewitt and the drugs I'd sold on campus because of his threats, and getting suspended from school, only to come face to face with the reality that a suspension was far from my punishment. I'd have to see Hewitt again in court. And I wouldn't lie to be on his side. I'd be in a battle with no armor, no air cover, and only my pleading, earnest words to set me free. Words that would implicate my own guilt. The whole realization felt freeing but damning at the same time. And it also felt like whatever my feelings were for Nico, it was over. It was over the moment Hewitt showed back up in my life. It had to be.

"What's that saying?" I started pacing the hotel carpet, "If you care about someone so much, you have to let them go? Set them free or whatever?"

"Fuck, Meredith, I'm not a poet. I don't know." Rhett cracked a smile and I smiled back even though I knew my eyes were sad, "I think of it more like this. You can't run from your past. You have to handle that shit. And you can't bring anyone else in to distract you or save you. That's not fair to anyone. So, handle your shit and then go from there. Was that poetic?"

"Ha, no," I scoffed, "but it's the truth. It's honest. So in that way, I guess so." Rhett walked over and gave me a quick hug, his arms feeling like steel cages around my body.

"You'll get through this, kid. Focus on you. Your dad and Nico and me, we will all understand." I nodded into his chest, but I wasn't so sure. He left as brusquely as he'd come in and I flopped onto the oversized hotel bed, staring up at the ceiling.

A KNOCK at the door broke my reverie and I wondered if Rhett had come back to talk more. My face was pink and water stained from rinsing it so many times in the ice cold water of the sink. I didn't bother looking through the peephole as I undid the latch.

Nico was standing in the doorway, one tan palm gripping the frame and the other hand in his joggers' pocket. I could only manage to blink up at him a few times, not knowing what to do. It was like Rhett was watching me, shaking his head no, reminding me of what we'd talked about and what we'd agreed to. Nico had to stay right here, in the hallway. Nothing good, even if it *felt good*, could come of letting him into my space when I knew I had to leave. That this had to end.

"Meredith, let me in." His voice was so gravelly and dark it made my stomach lurch. I opened the door wider and just like that he was in my room. So much for self-resolve.

"I want to ask you what the fuck happened tonight. Who Hewitt is and where I can find him so that I can bash his jaw in. I want to know what you're running from and why you won't let me or anyone else in. I want to know why you really agreed to this temporary tour manager job in the first place because I'm starting to think it has a hell of a lot more to do with what happened tonight than it does with your interest in professional fighting. And I want to know why you and your dad react to each other like strangers do." Nico ran both hands through his hair and let out a deep sigh, moving deeper in the hotel room and away from me. When he turned back around, his eyes were smoldering, a combination of lust and anger and frustration. And there was something else. Something like finality. Like a man who knew he'd lost but still had just a little bit of time left before that loss would become real. I saw that expression there because I knew it was also reflected on my own face.

"But you won't talk to me. You won't answer any of those questions, right?" I shook my head once to the side, confirming his response. He moved in closer, looming over me, good Nico and angry Nico warring within himself in a way that made him even hotter, even more electric, and I itched to reach out and touch him.

"Fine. Then don't talk. Don't say a fucking thing, Meredith. Just listen to me. Everything I say tonight, you'll listen. Yes?" I nodded my head affirmatively. I couldn't say no to Nico. Not when his words were like drugs and I was an addict, greedily soaking them up. Maybe he wanted to get something off of his chest, tell me that he was upset at how I'd distracted him too much during the beginning of his fighting career. Whatever he had to say, I wanted to hear it.

"Take off your clothes." Nico practically growled at me and for a moment I didn't move. Of all the things I expected him to say, that wasn't it. But when he cocked a dark eyebrow at me, indicating that he was getting impatient, I felt my hands move to the fabric of my cotton shirt and the denim of my jeans. I slid the clothing off, maintaining eye contact as best I could. My cheeks felt like they were on fire but still I wouldn't look away.

"Sit on the couch."

I moved over to the couch slowly, almost expecting him to tell me to do something else. But he stayed quiet, watching me intently as I sat on the couch, my back straight against the cushions and my ankles crossed.

"Spread your legs. Wider." I didn't move and Nico settled on the ground in front of me, lowering to his knees before resting back on his ankles. He stared up at me and his dimple appeared, but his eyes were still wicked, angry. "You're not listening, Meredith. You promised me you'd listen."

I spread my legs wider, slowly, and once they were wide enough, he lifted each ankle and rested one on each of his broad shoulders. I felt so exposed, so completely *his*. I started to shift myself, but it was nearly impossible with his thick, tan palms wrapped tightly around each ankle, his thumb gently stroking the delicate skin in a way that had my heart racing.

"Don't move." I couldn't move even if I wanted to, but the smirk on his face told me he already knew that. Then his face turned serious, liquid with heat as he unwrapped his hand from one of my ankles and started rubbing small circles on my most intimate parts. I still had my panties on, and he pushed the fabric delicately inside of me, the pressure so deliciously painful since I couldn't move in response. I was locked in place, by his hands and by his eyes, as he looked between my face and where he was touching me, tracking every little progression of my pleasure.

Nico stopped abruptly, grabbing both of my ankles in one large hand and sliding my panties down my legs. Once I was bare, he rested my ankles back on his shoulders and ducked his head, bringing his face to where his hand had been.

"Nico--"

"No talking," his lips brushed against the tender skin of my inner thigh, causing a shiver to break out over my body, "just listening, remember?" I nodded my head in agreement, but he couldn't see me. His tongue darted out and I couldn't keep the small moan from escaping my lips. It felt so hot, so intimate. When his tongue delved deeper, caressing over my skin from the inside out, I felt my legs start to tremble. He moved his hands back and forth between my calves and my inner thighs, massaging and grabbing my skin in a way that told me I wasn't the only one who was feeling desperate. He was my lifeline and I was his. I looked down at his dark head of hair, the sight almost throwing me over the edge, when he picked his eyes up to mine, his tongue still moving in and out of me. The intensity of his look, the relentless movement of his mouth and his hands had me unravelling at the seams. My legs started to shake harder, heat rushing to my core. I reached down and dug my hands into Nico's hair, a masculine growl escaping from the back of this throat as I pressed him even harder to me, his hands gripping my inner thighs and leaving little marks in my skin. It felt good, too good, and I started to see stars behind my eyelids as I squeezed my eyes shut and threw my head back in pleasure. My body felt like an electric wire that had finally snapped, the release spreading through me, making my limbs heavy and spent. When I finally opened my eyes, Nico was leaning back on his heels, his hands still caressing my inner thighs. His eyes were hooded and his lips slick with *me.* I started to sit up and squirm, but he gripped me tighter, forcing me to stay still and stare back at him.

"Turn around, grab the back of the couch." Nico finally spoke, his voice hoarse. I saw his hands going to the drawstring of his joggers and I quickly scrambled onto my knees with my forearms resting on the back of the couch. I had the very real fear that my limbs wouldn't be able to hold me up after my orgasm but I forced the thought down when I felt his warm, calloused hands wrap around my waist. He was standing now, leaning over my back, his lips at my ear. His breathing was ragged as his hands slid down my sides and over my ass, kneading my skin in a way that had me pushing myself back against him, my own neediness for his touch overriding any semblance of embarrassment or restraint.

I felt him at my entrance, the tension between our bodies blurring and combining until it felt like we both might snap if he didn't enter me. He slid in slowly, so slowly I wanted to scream for him to move in faster and harder and absolutely consume me. The groan that escaped his lips had me pushing back against him again, pulling him into me until he was completely seated, his front against my back.

"Fuck, Meredith." His lips brushed my ear as he spoke, his fullness filling me from the inside out. He started to move, pulling himself out slowly and then ramming back in. He kept up this pace, increasing it slightly until the rhythm became intoxicating. I started to feel another orgasm building again, my forearms and thighs starting to shake. Nico didn't miss a beat, reading my body perfectly, as he braced one palm over mine, and braced his other arm around my middle, holding me up and keeping me from falling into the couch's cushions.

"God, Nico..." my voice was quiet but powerful. He moved his head closer to mine and captured my lips in his, essentially shutting me up in the best way possible. He started to move faster, my orgasm crashing through me as he worked toward his own. After a final guttural groan, he pulled out of me and released himself on my back, the act like a permanent marking that required no words. His breathing started to calm down as I rested my head on my forearms, the combination of Nico's release and my own sweat settling into my skin.

I felt Nico's heat leave as he stood up and walked away from me, returning with a towel. He leaned back over, wiping my back clean and putting his lips against my ear.

"I won't say it, Meredith. I won't say it, but you know it. You feel it too. Your body tells me more than you ever will." He left my side and I slid down onto the couch, trying to unscramble his words. Was he saying we both knew this was goodbye? That this was the end? Or was he saying so much more? *Was he saying he loved me?* I wanted to ask, everything within me screaming to just say it. But I couldn't. I'd promised that I'd just listen. Nico started to pull on his clothes, me still naked on the couch except for my bra which neither of us had bothered with taking off. I felt frozen in place, wanting to leap up and hold him close to me, keeping his electricity and heat in my arms forever, but instead I didn't move. Nico gripped the hotel room door handle, hanging his head before turning around and facing me.

"See you tomorrow?" His voice was quiet and serious. I could tell by his tone and expression that he knew. He knew he wouldn't see me tomorrow. He knew that I knew it too. I nodded once, playing into the lie that we'd be able to just go on as we had been. Playing into the lie that this wasn't the end.

## 36

## MEREDITH

The view from the airplane window made me feel small, inconsequential. And that was good because I didn't want to think about Nico. About the look on his face when he turned and said "see you tomorrow?" before leaving my hotel room last night. It just hurt too much.

So instead, I thought about the clouds, the vast space that we can travel in a mere few hours, the warmth of the California sun that I was flying towards. I thought about these things so that I could think about *nothing. Anything.* But just not him.

"Prepare the cabin for arrival," the flight attendant's smooth voice cooed over the airplane speaker and I lifted my tray table, locking it in place. Ava had made flight arrangements for me late last night, texting me the details. Clearly she and Rhett had come up with a plan for me after the whole hallway fiasco with Hewitt. I wasn't angry. I was grateful. My pull towards Nico clouded my own judgment, and any ability to take the necessary adult steps. I'd live out the next two months of my suspension sentence back at home, my mother yelling and nitpicking at me but I didn't care. I had bigger things weighing on my mind than my disappointed mother.

When I landed, I collected my suitcase from baggage claim and checked it twice, remembering how I'd first met Nico when he'd picked me up to go back to the airport in Boston. How clueless had I been then about what that man would make me feel? I squash that thought down, *way down*, as I rolled my suitcase out into the warm, clear California air, closing my eyes and taking in a deep calming breath. Then I saw my mother's Mercedes, the entire scene playing out like deja vú in reverse from when she'd picked me up on campus after my suspension. She put the car in park and surprisingly got out, making her way onto the curb.

"Oh, Meredith," my mom wrapped her thin arms around me, her expensive bracelets clanging as she embraced me. I was so surprised that I didn't even hug her back. She helped me load my suitcases in the trunk before we both climbed in, the silence settling heavily over us.

"Are you hungry?" Her voice was bright, too bright, and I nodded my head no. A lump had suddenly settled in my throat, the unshed tears I'd been staving off since Nico left, since I left Nico, threatening to break loose.

"Honey," my mom cleared her throat, glancing nervously between the road and me, "we have to talk. You have to talk to me. Your dad," she cleared her throat again, "he's worried about you. I haven't heard him talk like that in years." She took on a wistful look, reflecting on memories I wasn't privy to as such a young child no doubt. "Just tell me what's going on and I will promise not to get mad, okay?" I could see the genuine concern on her face and I let out a long breath before sitting up straighter in my seat. I wouldn't tell her about Nico. I couldn't without risking a total and complete breakdown of the icy veneer I'd perfected over the last year. But I could tell her about Hewitt. I had to. It was now or never.

"I dated this guy...in college. We started dating a little over a year ago. He was smart and funny and a varsity athlete." I stopped and looked over at her. She gave me a reassuring nod to continue.

"Well, he was into some things that I didn't know about when we started dating. You know, drugs. And not just like weed. But bad stuff." I swallowed hard and then pressed on. "So one night, I went with him to a party. A lot of my friends were there, we were having fun. And it was the first time he offered us drugs. I'd never even seen Molly before. I mean, I'd heard about it and seen it in movies and stuff, but never in person. We all took some and then the rest of the night was...hazy. And at some point one of our friends, he didn't look so good. His face was ashy. I'll never forget how gray it was...it was just so dull." I stopped and glanced out the window, focusing everything in my being on the blurring trees along the side of the highway, trying to clear my mind of the memory.

"I told Hewitt that we should call for help. Call 911 or something. But Hewitt told me to relax and that I didn't know what I was talking about. And I was high, really high, so I just agreed. I danced with my friends, drank more. I was completely selfish. And then a few hours later, before we left, I looked back over at our friend Asher's gray face and it was even duller. Almost blue. His eyes were closed. And I just knew, mom, I just knew he was dead." I choked on the last work, feeling like I might vomit. My mom didn't say anything but she rested her delicate hand on my forearm, reassuring me.

"The next day when I asked Hewitt about it, he turned the whole thing on me. Twisting the story and my own memory, using my guilt to blame me. He told me that he'd tell if I didn't do something for him. I was so panicked, so unsure of myself that I agreed." I stopped and stared down at my lap. Unable to continue.

"Meredith, honey, please tell me. I'm not mad, I promise. I'm so proud of you for telling me what you've told me so far." Her words punched my gut and I looked up at her, incredulous.

"Proud? How could anyone be proud of me? I let a friend die and then sold drugs on campus, thinking that that would somehow make it right! I was being selfish, so worried about my own future that I incriminated myself again and I let Hewitt manipulate me. He promised, Mom, he promised that if I did this one thing it would all be over." My mom patted my forearm again, encouraging me to get the rest out. To be done with the secret once and for all.

"So, I sold the drugs on campus. Of course, I had no idea what I was doing and was a nervous wreck. A faculty member saw me and reported the incident. Which led to my suspension. But even then, Hewitt wasn't done. He kept dealing, kept getting himself deeper into that world. Our friend that died, I guess the autopsy came back and the authorities put the pieces together and--"

"They connected Hewitt to the accidental death, honey." My mom cut me off, finishing my sentence for me and I nodded in response.

"When I went to Dad's, I just wanted to run. From Hewitt, from my past, from my own guilt. So I agreed to the tour manager job. But Hewitt, he found me. And he wants me to go into a courtroom and lie for him. That's what he asked me to do. He said if I do this, *one last time*, then it will

really be over. But I know that's not true. And I can't keep
the lie any longer, Mom. I'm going to say that I was high.
That I knew our friend was dying and that I didn't call 911.
That I am partially to blame for his death."

My mom let out a deep breath and smiled at me, her
eyes watering. "I am so, so proud of you honey. I'm going to
help you get through this. Just keep telling the truth and we
will get through this, okay? You aren't alone with this
anymore I promise." I reached over and hugged her quickly,
before settling back in my seat. Tears flowed silent from my
cheeks and we didn't say anything else the rest of the way
home. I wasn't free yet, not completely, but I was one step
closer. And whatever the fallout, I was finally a little bit
proud of myself too.

When we pulled into the driveway, I noticed Toni's car
and a bunch of balloons tied to the front door. Toni came
bounding out, waving like a maniac, and I laughed with
happiness and relief.

"Red! Welcome back, my friend. I've missed you." Toni
pulled me into a ridiculous bearhug.

"Toni! I can't breathe." We both laughed and she
dragged me into the house, already blabbering about so
many random things that I couldn't keep up. It was good to
be home. Good to be here. But Nico's handsome face and
warm hands wedged their way back into my memory. It was
good to be home, but I'd never be the same without him.

## 37

## NICO

The next two weeks were a blur. Ava had officially stepped into Meredith's role and we'd traveled to six cities in fourteen days, four stops for fights and two for the press. I got my first loss but won the other three. I wasn't nearly as distraught as I should've been over the loss. I fought well, landed my punches, my opponent had just been more senior in his game. But that wasn't why it didn't affect me as much as it should have. It was because even though my body was very much here, present in the ring, my mind would wander. *To her.* I'd think about what she was doing right now, if she was talking to that Hewitt guy, if she'd ever come back. We haven't talked since that night. Since the night I'd said "see you tomorrow?" instead of truly saying goodbye.

Rhett and Ava didn't mention it either. They supported me in a strong and silent way, but everyone knew I was distracted. Still, I kept enough focus in the ring to bring my *almost* A-game every time. The press questions were getting easier. The flashes from cameras were becoming less jarring. I'd smile my crooked smile so that my dimple would appear and I'd answer the questions in the same coy but polite fashion that had become my *brand*, as Ava called it. It was a puppet show and I was grateful for the distraction. If this was going to be my life, the press was simply part of the gig, so it was better to get used to it early on.

Coach Barry had been distant ever since the hallway event. Rhett had fully stepped in as my Coach and Coach Barry just existed on the edges, occasionally critiquing me or meeting me ringside during a break between rounds, but it was different. Our relationship was cold. He apologized to me but I couldn't accept it. I'd never hurt his daughter in the way that he'd initially misinterpreted, but I had violated the trust Coach Barry had in me. It was awkward and embarrassing all around, so we just chose to put space between us and the honest conversations we should have had.

"Chavez, hit the shower! You have an interview in an hour and then we head to the airport." Rhett called out to me from the sparring mat and I nodded in acknowledgement. We'd been training all day, working on more complex combinations that would both give me a tactical advantage in the ring and please the crowd. This wasn't WWE fake shit, but you still wanted to have style and add entertainment value. That kept fans engaged and knocked the confidence off your opponent when you had the energy of the arena on your side. I jogged off the mat with a towel draped over my shoulder, heading toward the showers of the fancy training gym we'd been given access to during my time in New York.

"What do you mean she's going to court? Are you getting her a lawyer?" I stopped just shy of the entrance to the locker room when I heard Coach Barry's voice down a perpendicular hallway. The gym had a maze of hallways, connecting steam rooms and therapy rooms with showers and saunas. I couldn't see Coach Barry but I could hear him. His voice was hushed and worried and I knew I shouldn't eavesdrop but I couldn't help myself. I slowed my breathing and leaned my back against the cool, plaster wall, not making a sound.

"I mean, is there any way she could face jail time for that? All kids in college make dumb mistakes and she tried to do right by him--" Coach Barry was cutoff by whoever was speaking to him on the phone and my heart started to race at the thought of Meredith and jail time in the same sentence.

"Look, have we thought through all our options here? That's all I'm asking. I know I barely have a right, but she is my daughter--" He was cut off again and let out an exasperated sigh.

"Well, fine. But I want to be there. I want to show her that she's supported." He paused before continuing, "Yes of course I'm willing to miss a fight. She's my daughter. Are you seriously going to play that card again?" Even though I couldn't be sure, I'd bet money he was talking to Meredith's mother right now.

"It's on the 17th? Okay, yes, I'll be there. No, I'll get a hotel or sleep in my car before I stay at your house." He grumbled a few more things but I darted off quickly into the locker room, not wanting to risk Coach Barry noticing me.

He'd mentioned being there on the 17th which I assumed was some court date for Meredith for something I had no idea about, but probably involved that Hewitt motherfucker. I pulled out my phone and scrolled through my packed calendar. The 17th was a big match for me. Some opponent from Australia who was trying to make a name for himself in the North American circuit. I vaguely remembered Rhett briefing me on the guy.

There was no way I could miss the fight. Didn't matter if you were tired or sick, you fought. But I wanted to be there, for Meredith. Even if part of her didn't want me there. Her radio silence after she'd left told me that might be the case. But even if there was just the smallest part of her that would feel better or supported at having another face in that courtroom that wanted nothing but her to be free from whatever hell she's been through, then I should be there. I *had* to be there.

I turned the shower water to ice cold and let the stream slash painfully across my face, the eclectic feeling fading and resurfacing as water continued to flow. After a few minutes, I switched the temperature to warm and started to wash my hair, closing my eyes and seeing Meredith's beautiful red waves and the cute way her eyes crinkle around the corners when she laughed. God, that girl doesn't laugh enough. But she was so damn beautiful when she did.

Then it struck me. The thing I had to do. The realization irrevocably changed who I was as a fighter if I decided to go through with it. But it was almost like the decision was made when the idea came to mind. No internal debate necessary. I turned off the shower and towel dried, changing into a dress shirt and dark brown slacks that Ava had helped me pick out for today's interview. I put on my new fancy cufflinks and brushed down my wet, wayward hair in the mirror.

I was going to do this. Do it for her. Even if it damned me.

~

THE INTERVIEW WAS EASY ENOUGH. My responses were short and smooth, just how Ava had coached me, and I found myself drifting mentally during the entire thing. It was easy to do since the questions were always the same, asking me about my career goals, who I thought my biggest challenge would be, if I was ready for the next fight. I'd learned the key was to give a bunch of coy non-answers but still provide enough insight to appease the crowd. I didn't want to start any serious rivalries or stir the pot. Wasn't my style. Just wanted to show up, fight solidly, and win. Well, except for *right now*. Right now, I wanted to risk throwing all of that away for Meredith.

After the interview, I exited through the back, Ava waiting for me with a black car and the memory of Meredith standing there instead of her came crashing back to me. Even though Ava was just as pretty, and arguably way more friendly, she wasn't Meredith. No one was.

"Nice job tonight, Nico. You're really getting the hang of this. You're going to be a star." Ava punched my shoulder and I smiled at her, genuinely grateful for all of her help.

"Thanks, I appreciate it."

"So we will head back to the hotel to get our things and then head to the airport after a quick dinner." Ava smiled and glanced back down at her phone. I shifted slightly in my seat before making my resolve final.

"I think I may head back to the training gym, catch a ride to the airport from there." I kept my words calm, casual. I didn't need Ava suspecting anything.

"You've trained all day, Nico. Aren't you tired? You should eat." Ava cocked her head at me, confused but not suspicious.

"I just have a lot of energy today, you know? I'll eat when we land."

"Another room service pizza?" She raised her eyebrows at me and then laughed. She must have seen my room service bills. The thought reminded me of Meredith again, but these days every little thing did.

"You know me well."

"Okay well, just don't tire yourself out too much. You have a lot of matches coming up over the next two week sprint." I nodded, giving her a closed-lip smile. If I had it my way, I'd be having a few less matches on the horizon, specifically on the 17th.

When we got back to the hotel, I didn't bother changing. I called an Uber and went back to the training gym, the space largely empty minus a few staff members rearranging equipment and cleaning the space. I made my way to a punching bag, rolling up my dress shirt sleeves and going through the sequence in my mind.

When you watch fighters it's easy to think that they just throw their firsts, hard and straight, at their opponent. That it's just brute force, aggressive effort, and no skill. But every tendon, every small bone in the arm, from bicep to pinky, has to be perfectly and properly aligned. If not, you risk more than just not landing a solid punch. You risk injury. The kind of injury that can radiate pain up through your entire arm and down your back. The kind of injury that can have you sidelined for days or weeks. The kind of injury that every fighter spends years and hours on the mat with coaches trying to avoid. The kind of injury that I was about to inflict on myself.

I braced my legs but not perfectly. I struck out my fist a few times, locking my elbow and not rotating my wrist. For a moment I felt like my novice self again. The me who was fighting for a few hundred bucks to try and feed my sisters that week. The me who had no clue, no guidance, just raw unrelenting energy and desperation. It was just a simple movement, an amateur punch, that reminded me of just how far I'd come. I settled into that groove, repeating the flawed movement gently at first and then more aggressively. I had to actively retrain my brain towards bad habits. I picked up the pace, hitting harder and harder, feeling the warning signs tingle through my fist and up into my forearm, the signs that usually would tell a fighter to stop, reposition and try again. Except I didn't stop. I leaned harder into the mistake, punching the bag with every ounce of frustration I felt about Meredith.

"Fuck!" I let out a painful growl, trying to keep my voice low so I didn't draw any attention. There was a pop and then just blind, white pain. My fingers started to swell and my wrist was turned in an unnatural position. There was no way to know if it was a break or a strain. But it was definitely not good. Which is exactly what I wanted.

I cradled my hand against my chest, using my other hand to call another Uber. The pain was real and white hot. I took several long breaths and blew them out of my nose, trying to stay as calm as possible. But even through the pain, through the natural fear coursing within my body that I had injured my most valuable asset, that I had just risked literally everything I'd spent the past several years working and praying for, I felt no regret. She was worth it.

## 38

## MEREDITH

The suit jacket and matching slacks that my mother had forced me into felt suffocating. I pulled at the sides of the jacket, my hands clammy with nerves. Never in my life did I think I'd be having to do this. But here we were. And in a matter of a few hours this part would all be over. The scariest part was not knowing what would come after that.

For the past two weeks, Toni had been my absolute rock. My mom had hired me a lawyer and she'd coached me on how to tell my truth. It was incredibly frightening to think about retelling the entire event of that night and the fallout, but it was far scarier to think about lying. I already told myself that once I sat down at the stand, I would take a deep breath and block out the room. It would just be my truth and me.

"Dude, I'll be right there in the courtroom the whole time. You just look out and stare at me and I'll make a stupid face so that you almost lose your shit up there." Toni whispered in my ear as we ascended the courthouse steps and I laughed but it only made my nerves that much more obvious. My mother patted my shoulder reassuringly as we entered the courtroom, the huge wooden doors spreading wide with formality. We were early and I went up to the front to meet with my lawyer. She was short and stocky, absolutely no nonsense and immediately instilled trust in you that she wouldn't let shit get out of control.

"We've been over this. Now, it's all you. Are you feeling good?" She squared my shoulders, almost having to look up at me due to her short height.

"Not sure about good..." I swallowed hard, my mouth suddenly too dry,

"Well, good enough will do. Just don't choke up there. And don't forget your facts. Just stick to the facts. When you're telling the truth, the only thing that can trip you up is your own nerves." I nodded at her and took a seat in the stiff wooden chair, alternating between clasping and unclasping my hands. Apparently Hewitt had been in court for days since he was facing several serious drug charges. The thought of seeing him here, the first time since he accosted me in the hallway after Nico's fight, made a shiver run up my spine. I hoped, prayed, that after today I'd never have to see that fucker again.

I heard more and more people arrive but I kept staring straight ahead. Once the judge entered, then the whole thing would officially start and I just kept my eyes on the judge's stand like nothing else existed. I didn't want to turn back and see Toni making a funny face or my mother smiling comfortingly. I feared it would make me break down with nerves and tears. I needed to remain stoic and collected. I tried to harness as much of that energy from my lawyer sitting next to me who looked like she may as well have been at the DMV and not sitting in a courtroom with a client who was about to testify.

Finally the judge entered, the whole thing feeling like a movie playing out in front of me. He was draped in black and nodded once at the room before ascending to his seat. Next, Hewitt and his lawyer entered. He was wearing a navy blue suit, looking every bit the privileged varsity athlete that he was. For a moment I couldn't take my eyes away. I sat there frozen, staring at him, remembering the first time we'd met on campus and thinking how there was no way in hell I could've imagined then that our last meeting would be like this.

"All rise!" The judge bellowed out and the room stood and then sat again when the judge did. My legs felt like they were vibrating, they were so shaky.

"Today we are here with regards to the case of Hewitt Langston vs. California, facing several counts of drug distribution and money laundering as well as involvement in unintentional manslaughter. We have a witness here today, Miss Meredith Barry, on account of the death of Asher Midland due to drug distribution and overdose. Do both of you understand the charges being discussed today and why you are here to testify?"

"I do." My voice felt like sandpaper as I nodded at the judge and Hewitt repeated after me before the judge removed his reading glasses.

"Miss Barry, please take the stand to give your account of the evening of October 8th, 2020 in reference to the charges against Hewitt Langston regarding Asher Midland." My lawyer nodded firmly at me and I rose to my feet, barely making my way over to the stand.

"Do you solemnly swear to tell the whole truth and nothing but the truth so help you God?" I raised my right hand, my vision blurring with the rush of blood and nerves throughout my head.

"I do."

After uttering those two small but meaningful words I finally glanced out at the crowd, any sounds drowned out by the blood pumping in my ears. I spotted Toni next to my mother and she winked at me. I noticed my dad sitting in the row behind them, looking just as uncomfortable as I was in a suit. I hadn't even known he'd be here and the thought sent a warm flush through my chest. I'd worried that our relationship had been ruined before it even really started by what had happened on Nico's tour, but here he was. Looking very fatherly and supportive. I gave him a small smile and he smiled back, his eyes looking worried but proud.

I was about to glance back down at the wooden surface of the stand when I briefly swung my glance over to the other side of the courtroom. I did a double take when I saw a tan, handsome face near the back, only a few feet from the door. He was slouched on the bench, nearly taking up half of it with his tall, strong body. When I glanced back he was still there, not just a figment of my rampant and nerve-ridden imagination. He smiled at me slowly, that damn dimple appearing in his cheek and I felt like it was just the two of us suspended in space--

"Miss Barry, all you alright? Are you good to proceed?" The sound of the judge's voice brought me back to the stiff chair digging into my back and the courtroom filled with expectant faces staring at me. How long had I been zoned out staring at Nico? What the hell was he doing here? I couldn't answer any of the questions flooding through my mind, but his presence calmed me. A warmth settled over my cool, goosebump ridden skin and I cleared my throat to respond.

"Yes, your honor. Sorry."

"Alright then. Please tell us every detail you can recall

from the evening of October 8th, 2020." I swallowed past the lump in my throat and let out a deep breath. This was it. This was actually happening. I almost felt like I blacked out as the words began to flow past my lips, my past several months of desperation slowly alleviating from my shoulders one bit at a time as I told my honest account of what happened that evening and the guilt I felt for not doing more for Asher. I didn't look at Hewitt when I mentioned him by name, recalling how when I'd asked him to call 911 he told me to relax and when I brought it up to him the next day he shifted the blame onto me. I recounted feeling black-mailed into selling drugs on campus but openly admitted that I could've taken about a dozen other courses of action than blindly following through and expecting it to actually end Hewitt's hold over me. I wasn't the victim, but I had still been lied to and used.

When I finished speaking, I glanced between my lawyer and the judge. My lawyer gave me a reassuring nod and her face looked pleased. I felt a huge surge of relief at her confident expression.

"Thank you Miss Barry. Does this conclude your account?"

"It does, your honor."

"You may return to your counsel."

I rose on less shaky legs and went to sit beside my lawyer, finally glancing over at Hewitt. His face was red with anger, the veins in his neck protruding, making his suit collar look painfully tight. I didn't smirk or smile. This wasn't a victory. This was an absolution. This was a step towards freedom. I didn't want to damn or ruin Hewitt. I wanted to forget him.

"Legal counsel, please approach the bench." The judge glanced up and both lawyers stood to head to his podium. I could feel Hewitt glaring daggers at me but I stared straight ahead, ready for this to be over. Ready for whatever responsibility or due the judge felt I deserved.

"Miss Barry, please rise. This court finds you not guilty in association with Hewitt Langston's charge of unintentional manslaughter of Asher Midland due to overdose. However, I may suggest being smarter about the company you keep and the decisions you make. Let this be your warning and not a habit. Do you understand?"

"I do, your honor." My voice cracked in relief on the last word and the rack of his gavel against wood was the sound of my new start.

"This courtroom is released for recess. Miss Barry and counsel, you are free to go. Mr. Langston and council, we will resume in one hour." The judge rose from his podium and left the room before others started to rise from their seats.

"Good work, Meredith. Real nice work." My lawyer padded my arm and then finished stacking her papers. I followed her down the courtroom hallway and into the lobby.

"Oh, Meredith!" My mom pulled me into her arms, nearly suffocating me, "I'm so, so proud of you sweetheart." She had tears at the corners of her eyes and I patted her back, trying to loosen her deathgrip.

"Thanks, mom. And thank you for helping me get a lawyer, she was great." When she finally released me, I noticed my father standing awkwardly a few feet away, like he couldn't decide if he should approach me or not. I closed the distance between us, embracing him in an initially awkward hug.

"Thanks for being here, Dad." He wrapped his arms around my back, a sigh escaping his throat.

"Of course, sweetheart. I'm so sorry you had to go through all of that and that I haven't been there--"

"It's okay, Dad. Really, it is." I cut him off, not wanting to make him feel guilty or regretful at this moment. He'd taken time away from tour and made an effort to be a real father during one of the hardest moments of my life. I couldn't ask for more.

The thought of my dad leaving the fighting tour and his trainees in the gym brought Nico back to my memory, the flurry of commotion following the end of the deposition distracting me. I pulled out of my father's arms, glancing around the lobby for any sign of Nico.

"Who are you looking for, sweetheart?" My dad looked at me, confused.

"Nico. Where did he go?"

"Nico? Nico's here?" My dad's eyebrows nearly flew off the top of his forehead and he started to glance around even more aggressively than I had been.

"You didn't know Nico was here?" My voice was thin, confused. *How could Nico be here and my dad not know?*

Then I spotted him, just outside the courthouse front doors, the sun streaming down on his olive skin as he leaned against a column, looking at his phone. That's when I noticed a white cast on his right hand and wrist and my heart rate spiked in my chest. Without saying another word to my dad, I moved quickly toward the front doors, throwing them open.

## 39

# NICO

"Nico!" Meredith caught me off guard and I stood up straight, almost dropping my phone. "What happened to your hand, are you alright?" She took the cast around my wrist gently in her hand and looked up at me, genuine surprise and concern on her pretty face.

"Oh yeah, it's nothing. Just a sprain. Should be fine in another week." I shrugged casually at her, not needing to mention the fact that I'd gotten this injury in order to be here in this exact moment: the moment where I finally got to tell her how I feel after her courtroom deposition. Rhett had been fucking furious, but his blood boiled a little less when we learned from the x-ray that it was only a 3-week healing period. Exactly what I'd been going for. Rhett had waxed poetic for hours about the importance of technique which ironically was the only reason I even knew how to so perfectly inflict this kind of injury, because he'd taught me so well in the first place.

"But doesn't that throw off your whole schedule? I mean you were supposed to be in at least three fights this week--"

"Meredith, it's fine," I cut her off, admiring how sharp

her memory was about my tour dates, "I'm exactly where I want to be." I lowered my voice, leaning in closer to her, my lips above her ear. Her facial expression changed, and she tilted her head, a small sweet smile curving her lips.

"I didn't expect you to be here. How did you even know?" I laughed and looked down at the ground, not wanting to get into the details of how I'd eavesdropped on her dad's phone call and laid out this entire reckless plan. It didn't change how much I was itching to get back in the ring, how much I realized I loved the feeling of fighting and winning and was even growing to like the chaos of the media and the interviews. But I wanted Meredith too. I needed her by my side.

"You killed it up there. That's not an easy thing to do, Meredith. You never cease to impress me." Meredith blushed and looked down at her hands.

"That was nothing compared to what you do on tour. I mean, there must've been only like forty people in that courtroom and it still made me want to throw up. I don't know how you perform like that in front of thousands of people without freaking out."

I moved in closer to her, my lips right at her ear, the smell of her gorgeous hair flooding my nostrils, "Don't tell anyone but sometimes I definitely freak out. Nearly pissed myself the first night on tour I was so nervous," she giggled and leaned in impossibly closer, "but then I looked out and saw you in the front row, the only person there supporting me even if you didn't know it at the time. I knew that today, I owed you that. I owed you my support when you looked out at the crowd." I kissed her neck, just below her ear, gently. It was barely a kiss at all, a fraction of what I actually wanted to do to her. But it was enough. I could hear her breathing pick up. She lifted her face up, her eyes meeting mine. I bent down towards her lips--

"Nico." I stopped short when I heard Coach Barrys' voice bark out. He was standing about three feet away, his hands in his slacks' pockets. I'd known the man for two years and had never seen him in anything other than gym sweats and t-shirts. His whole body was stiff but he didn't look as angry as he looked cautious, assessing. I moved away from Meredith as she glanced nervously between us.

"Coach." I cleared my throat and nodded at him. He moved his gaze slowly down to my wrist and then to Meredith, finally landing back on me. We stared at one another for several long moments, the connection we'd built as fighter and coach allowing us to communicate without words. He knew. The realization settled calmly over his face. He knew that I'd done this to be here. With her. With his daughter. He took a step forward and I felt my thighs brace reflexively. I was preparing for him to strike a punch.

Instead, he stuck out his hand in the most fatherly move I'd ever seen. For a moment I didn't move, not believing if it was really happening. But when he held his ground I reached out awkwardly with my left hand since my right was still cradled in a cast. I shook his hand and tried to convey with my eyes how much I cared about her. How I'd never let anyone, or anything, hurt her like that Hewitt asshole had. Coach Barry gave me a firm nod as his only response and then kissed Meredith gently on the cheek.

"See you at your mother's, sweetheart." He jogged down the steps, rubbing his palm over his bald scalp as he headed toward the parking lot.

"Well, that was awkward." Meredith laughed lightly, rubbing her hands down her arms. She didn't even know just how awkward it was, your coach knowing you risked your most valuable asset for his only daughter. But I'd do it again. Ideally, I'd never have to. Meredith would be mine. I didn't respond to her comment. I moved in quickly, threading my left hand into her hair, the hair I'd spent so many nights dreaming about and pulled her lips to mine. I crashed into her, pouring all the frustration and passion that I had for her with my mouth and tongue. She met me halfway, her hands crawling up my back and into the back of my hair. I pressed her back up against the cool marble of the courthouse, not relenting.

"Um, hi" I braced my palm flat against the wall, breaking my lips from Meredith's when I heard a throat cleaning, "you must be Nico. I'm Toni. And we are in a very public place so perhaps we could continue this," she gestured to Meredith and me, a funny smirk on her face, "elsewhere."

"Um, yeah," Meredith smoothed her hair, shooting a quick smile at me that promised more of *this* later. "Nico, Toni, Toni meet Nico."

"Barely any introduction necessary," Toni patted my shoulder and I couldn't help but laugh. She was small and spunky, her energy reminding of a rookie fighter with no fear. "Who's hungry? Because I for one am freaking starving." Toni locked arms with Meredith and I followed them down the courthouse steps.

"Meet me back at my mom's?" Meredith looked back at me and I nodded. We needed more time together. First for feeling and then for talking.

"Yeah, text me the address." Her face was bright as she and Toni piled into a fancy Mercedes and sped off.

MEREDITH @ 1:15 PM: 4251 Rosewood Lane.

.   .   .

Nico @ 1:16 PM: I'll be there.

AFTER LUNCH at her mom's, Meredith excused us and led me out back toward a fancy looking guesthouse. Meredith definitely grew up lightyears away from how I'd been raised and even her dad looked uncomfortable throughout lunch but he and her mother managed to keep it civil for the sake of Meredith and all that she'd been through today. The grass was soft and damp and licked at our heels as she led me through the yard and quickly unlocked the door to the guest house.

Once we were inside, it felt quiet. Between Toni and her mother, lunch had been quite the entertaining commotion, with my only contributions being a few head nods here and there. Meredith sat down on the edge of the bed, her cheeks rosy and her feet bare and her hair a little wild. She looked like some forest princess, a creature so beautiful that I feared if I closed my eyes she'd vanish when I opened them again.

"Do you...want to talk?" She licked her lips, her eyes wide.

"Yes..." I moved toward her, leaning over her body and placing my palms on the bed, the soft surface bearing the weight of my right wrist. "But not until after I do this." I locked my lips over hers, kissing her more gently this time. We had time. It was just us. I could savor her like she deserved. I wrapped my left hand around her lower back, lifting her up slightly and then lowering her back down on the bed, my body covering hers. I ran my left hand down the side of her body, resting on my right forearm. She let out the sexiest sigh and I swore I'd remember that sound for the rest of my life.

"I missed you." She breathed into my neck as I ran my hand under her shirt over her bare stomach.

"How much?" I growled into her neck, massaging her breasts over her bra.

"A lot." Her voice was whispery.

"Multiply a lot by ten." Before she could respond I kissed her again and unzipped my jeans, grinding my hips into her. I felt her reach down and undo the button of her slacks, shimmying inefficiently to try and get them off. Our movements were short and sloppy as we worked to remove our clothes, Meredith laughing at me as she helped take off my shirt since my cast was giving me a hard time. When we were finally naked, I laid her back down, wedging myself between her thighs and grinding my hips against her skin. The feeling was so powerful, so insanely intoxicating that it felt even better than feeling your opponent up against the ropes.

"Nico, please. Now. I need you." Meredith pushed her hips off the mattress, trying to meet mine. I braced myself at her entrance, locking my eyes with hers as I entered slowly, not letting out a sigh until I was fully immersed, her body gripping perfectly around mine like we were made for each other.

"You're. Mine. Meredith." I ground into her, matching each word with a thrust. Now that she was free from her past, there was nothing that could keep me from her. I could feel her body tightening around mine, sweet moans escaping her throat. Before she found her release, I flipped our positions, settled her on top of me, my head up against the headboard. She took a moment to find her balance, feeling me fully beneath her. She gripped my biceps, riding me at her own rhythm, bringing us both to the brink of release.

"You're mine too." Meredith's voice was barely above a whisper as she threw her head back and let go, my hips pounding into her until I came shortly after. Her sweaty forehead collapsed onto my shoulder and I held her against my chest.

"Do we talk now?" After a few minutes she looked up at me, her face rosy and hooded, a satisfied smile on her lips. I brushed away a few strands of her dark red hair, tucking them behind her ear.

"Pizza first?" I gave her my best megawatt smile and she laughed, pushing against my chest.

"Is all you think about pizza?"

"Sometimes I think about steak. Or burgers. Never sweets though. Don't have much of a sweet tooth." She laughed again, feigning frustration with me.

"When's your next fight?" She settled beside me, running her fingers down my chest.

"Ten days out in Phoenix. You coming?"

"Yeah. Can I bring Toni? She's been dying to go to a match since this whole thing started." I laughed picturing little Toni jumping up and down, screaming at the ring. She'd be a natural.

"I think we can get her a seat. I know a guy." Meredith laughed again and kissed me. Not in a passionate way but in the way that people do when they kiss all the time. When they're together, like it was a habit.

## 40

## MEREDITH (6 MONTHS LATER)

Cool air blasted through vents in the arena causing goosebumps to break out over my arms. I knew I should've worn a jacket but in my defense it would have ruined my outfit: a baby blue dress that contrasted well with my dark red hair. I knew Nico would be looking out at me from the ring tonight, the first time we'd seen each other in a few weeks, and I wanted to take his breath away. But not too much, you know, since he was about to fight a serious opponent and all.

"This. Is. Awesome." Toni marveled next to me, staring around at the breadth and expanse of the arena as guests found their seats. Our dinner ended early so we were here before most, giving us some prime time people watching. This wasn't Toni's first match on Nico's tour. She'd been joining me at several other fights over the past few months, but she never failed to entertain with her genuine excitement. During Nico's California stop, we'd surprised Toni's brother with seats and watching the two of them react to the fight was almost more entertaining than the fight itself. Almost.

"Hey girls, settling in okay? Need anything?" Amelia, Nico's new tour manager made her way down our aisle, her iPad in hand. I had to admit that I'd been entirely wrong about Amelia. She was down to earth and awesome, grew up near the ring since her dad was also a coach and they'd been close. She made sure Nico got where he needed to go and had what he needed to succeed. I actually felt way more comfortable during our weeks apart, when I was at school and he was traveling on tour, knowing she had his back.

"All good, never been better." Toni wiggled her eyebrows and kept snapping pictures with her phone, no doubt sharing them on Instagram or with her brother.

"Glad to hear it. Tonight should be an interesting one. I mean, we know our boy Nico is good but his opponent is on the rise also. And he's a cocky fucker."

Toni snorted in response to Amelia's harsh words and I fidgeted in my seat. I'd only seen Nico lose once and it wasn't fun. I hated knowing that he would beat himself up about it in the hotel room after, replaying each round in his head to try and improve and figure out what he could have done better. I mean, it was part of the sport but it was still hard sitting by his side, knowing there was nothing you could do to make the person you cared about the most feel better.

"I'm gonna go get Celeste, she's here tonight. Her first time seeing her brother on the main stage." Amelia smiled at us before scuttling off. I swear I never saw that woman sit down. Even during the matches she usually stood at the edge of the VIP front row section, working away on her iPad, taking calls, or conversing with my dad or Rhett before hurrying off to complete some other task.

"Who's Celeste?" Toni didn't look at me when she asked

the question, her eyes glued on her phone as she created some witty caption for her latest Instagram post.

"Nico's oldest sister. I've never met her before, only talked to her a few times on Facetime when I've been with Nico." A flush of nerves flooded my stomach. I knew that Nico and I were solid and meant to be with each other, but I hadn't met his sisters yet and they were the only family he ever talked about. He cared about them so much. *What if Celeste didn't like me?*

"Dude, relax" Toni patted my thigh, "she's younger than you. That's like a million times easier than having to meet an older sister." She spoke like she had profound knowledge on the topic which made zero sense but I was grateful for her confidence nonetheless.

A few minutes later, Amelia returned with Celeste. She was even prettier in person, her olive skin and long dark hair looking just like Nico's. But she had pale green eyes that were way more pronounced from a few feet away than over a video chat. She wasn't even eighteen but she was already curvy and feminine, her hips swaying as she made her way down our aisle behind Amelia.

"Ohmygosh, Meredith! It's so nice to finally meet you in person." Celeste embraced me in a hug, leaning over since I was still seated. I was surprised by her warmth but then again I was always still a bit icy around new people, overly concerned that I'd do or say something embarrassing. Celeste didn't seem shy at all, her warm electric energy reminding me again of Nico. I introduced her to Toni and then she took the seat next to me, flipping all of her black wavy hair over one shoulder.

"I've never seen him fight like this before! I'm kinda nervous, is that normal?"

"Totally. I get nervous every time," I laughed and she made a face like 'thank goodness it's not just me' before pulling a tube of lip gloss out of her purse and swiping it across her full lips.

"Nico says you're back in college, right? When do you graduate?"

"Yeah, I've been back for a few months. I'm on track to graduate early so hopefully I'll be done in another year." I smiled shyly at Celeste and Toni leaned over me.

"She's a genius. She just never likes to tell anybody that so I do it for her."

"Ignore her." I shoved Toni's shoulder playfully and we all stopped talking when the lights started to dim and the music flared up.

"They do that when the match is close to starting." I whisper yelled at Celeste who nodded in response, not taking her eyes off the spotlit stage.

"Ladies and gentlemen...welcome to tonight's premiere event, to the place that everyone in this city wants to be!" The crowd roared in response and Celeste gripped her hand to her chest in surprise at the noise. It was like watching myself at my first fight all over again.

"Our first opponent for this evening's match is not your typical brawler, my friends. He is a pretty boy. A party boy. A man of privilege and ego. Please welcome to the ring, the one, the only...Ethan Grable!" The crowd erupted in a mix of cheers and boos as the spotlight swiveled to the right and a tall, insanely ripped hooded man made his way into the ring. When he threw off his blue silk cap, his blonde hair reflected brightly under the stage lights, electric blue eyes staring out at the crowd. He had a similar figure to Nico, strong and intimidating, but still lithe and athletic. He didn't have any tattoos or gnarly scars like most of the fighters did. He looked like a preppy, perfect Cali boy.

"Woah." Celeste let out a breath and I laughed when I looked over at her. "Are all the fighters this hot?" Her eyes went wide and then she looked back at me, "Wait, don't answer that. I don't want to hear about my brother, ew." I laughed at her response and pretended to be zipping my lips. Because of course I thought her brother was freaking hot. The hottest.

Ethan looked out at the crowd like he loved being admired. He was confident and cocky, just as the announcer had described. Every bit the pretty playboy you'd imagine.

"And now, my good friends, the man of the moment, the fighter on the rise...let's give it up for Nico Chavez!" The crowd erupted again, Ethan pandering into it, baiting the crowd to scream louder like he loved the controversy. Like he didn't even care if the crowd loved Nico more; that only fueled his excitement. I swallowed past the nerves of remembering what Amelia had said, about this being a tightly paired match, and waited for Nico to emerge from his corner.

Nico approached the ring more calmly, more reserved. When he slipped off his red silk cap he looked out, finding our section, and smiled that insanely hot boyish smile that made me fall in love all over again. He almost looked shy, just his charm.

"This is so freaking weird!" Celeste squealed next to me and gripped my hand, but I kept my eyes locked with Nico's. Whatever happened tonight, in this fight or the next, he was mine and I was his. We'd get through it, together. I could feel his warmth, his electricity pulling me toward him and I leaned forward in my seat just to soak it in.

The bell chimed out, the bright sound reverberating throughout the arena, signaling the start of round one. This was my new normal, my new happy place, supporting Nico just like he had supported me. Nothing from my past could hurt me now.

## 41

## CONCLUSION

Thank you so much for reading the second book in my fighter series, *Against The Ropes!* If you haven't already read *In His Corner*, be sure to check it out as it's the first book in the series but each can still be read as standalone :)

Up next...the third and final book in my fighter series...*Below The Belt!*

What will happen a few years after the end of *Against The Ropes* when Nico Chavez's sister, Celeste, lands a coveted PR internship for celebrity clients? For the past few years, Celeste has been living in her older brother's shadow as he's risen to fame as a top fighter.

She can't wait to embark on her own professional life when she lands the PR internship of her dreams. But when Celeste learns that her client is none other than Ethan

Grable, her brother's biggest opponent in the ring, she'll be forced to choose between family and career.

Ethan Grable isn't like most of his opponents. He didn't start by fighting in the streets. Ethan is the son of a former professional athlete and has lived a life of privilege...and insurmountable pressure to succeed. His spoiled-rotten, party boy reputation is his outlet, and he has no problem playing into it.

When Ethan finds out that his summer tour PR manager is a gorgeous young woman, he has zero complaints. But when he finds out that Celeste is actually Nico Chavez's younger sister, he has a choice to make. And knowing Ethan, it's not going to be the honorable one.

Will Celeste choose family loyalty over professional opportunity? And will Ethan choose honesty over playing with fire?

*Below the Belt* coming Summer 2021!

Instagram and TikTok: @skaragray

Website: www.skaragray.com - sign up for my newsletter and get the latest updates!

## 42

## ABOUT THE AUTHOR

Skara Gray began writing after her avid love of reading led her to want to create characters and stories of her own. She writes in the mornings, evenings, and weekends, enjoying bringing fresh takes to well-loved tropes with highly dynamic and compelling characters. She regularly releases new works, so be sure to keep an eye out for the next exciting story!

To FIND out more about Skara Gray or her books, explore the links below:

Amazon Page

Website

Newsletter

Goodreads Page

Wattpad

Instagram

Printed in Great Britain
by Amazon